The Discreet Lesbian™
Mandy Book 1

Mackenzie Stone

PUBLISHED BY:
Lanie Dills Publishing
Copyright © 2012
ISBN: 0916744051a

http://TheDiscreetLesbian.com

****

This is a work of fiction. Names, characters, places, and incidents are products of the author's imagination or are used fictitiously and are not to be construed as real. Any resemblance to actual events, locales, organizations, or persons, living or deceased, is entirely coincidental.

****

The Discreet Lesbian™

The Discreet Lesbian™ 1
Mandy Book 1 1
Mandy Episode 1 4
Chapter 1...4
Chapter 2...8
Chapter 3...12
Chapter 4...15
Chapter 5...18
Chapter 6...21
Chapter 7...24
Chapter 8...28
Chapter 9...30
Chapter 10..32
Chapter 11..34
Mandy Episode 2 37
Chapter 1...37
Chapter 2...40
Chapter 3...41
Chapter 4...44
Chapter 5...46
Chapter 6...50
Chapter 7...54
Chapter 8...57
Chapter 9...59
Chapter 10..61
Chapter 11..64
Chapter 12..66
Mandy Episode 3 68
Chapter 1...68
Chapter 2...73
Chapter 3...76
Chapter 4...79
Chapter 5...83
Chapter 6...87
Chapter 7...89
Chapter 8...90

Chapter 9..92
Chapter 10..94
Chapter 11..97
Chapter 12..100
Chapter 13..102
Mandy Episode 4 105
Chapter 1..105
Chapter 2..108
Chapter 3..110
Chapter 4..114
Chapter 5..116
Chapter 6..118
Chapter 7..121
Chapter 8..123
Chapter 9..125
Chapter 10..128
Chapter 11..130
Thank You! 134

Mandy Episode 1

2012 — My name is Amanda Carol Blackwood Allen. I am a lesbian. This is my story ...

Chapter 1
Early 1960s

It was a little strange because Kathleen had never done anything like this before. I opened my front door and she was standing there. Even though I wasn't expecting company and was naturally a little flustered, I found myself thrilled to see my friend. She asked matter-of-factly, "Hi Mandy, I was on my way home from school and thought I would drop by for a few minutes, is that okay?"

Kathleen was older than me, a college student and had her own apartment close to campus. The university she attended was near enough, however, that she came back home on the weekends.

I blinked at first and then replied, "Of course, come on in," as I stepped aside.

Kathleen was acting curious. She asked to come in yet hesitated on my porch before entering. Then she took one step inside the door, stopped and just stood there, looking at me as she did sometimes at church when she thought I didn't notice. She was staring directly into my eyes and it was piercing. I couldn't pull my eyes away from hers. After what seemed like forever but was only a few seconds, I managed to ask her softly if she wanted to sit down. I was a bit overtaken by her intensity, and I was also beginning to realize that this impromptu visit was not just a friendly little Friday afternoon call on a casual acquaintance.

Kathleen said, "Okay, yes," and sat down in a green overstuffed armchair that was close to the kitchen door. Her eyes never left mine as she sat there. She wasn't actually saying anything, but her presence was charging the room with a pulsating energy. Her deep green eyes were steady on me and revealed a determined purpose. They unmasked me and drilled straight through to my soul to a truth unknown to me but that existed within me.

Rattled by the way she was looking at me I finally managed to ask her if she would like something to drink. She answered as commonplace as could be, "Yes, that would be great," but I detected an almost imperceptible edge to her voice that I was certain I had never heard before as she spoke those few everyday words.

I walked toward the kitchen glad for something to do. I needed a momentary reprieve from the overpowering energy in the living room. As I passed by her chair, however, Kathleen reached out, grabbed my hand and pulled me down onto her lap. Almost in the same motion, she gently took my face into her hands and kissed me tenderly, softly, sweetly right on my lips for the longest moment.

She released my face and admitted, "Mandy, that was something I've wanted to do for a very, very long time. Did you feel something too?"

I couldn't answer her. I wanted to but I couldn't. Startled, confused and definitely speechless, my wits momentarily left me. At that point, I was doing good just to keep my legs under me. I never thought about something like that being on Kathleen's mind. Nevertheless, it took less than a tenth of a split second for me to know beyond a shadow of a doubt that I felt plenty in that kiss; I felt damn plenty.

In fact, I'd never felt anything like that in my life. The suddenness of the kiss, while shocking, didn't diminish the instant connection I felt. But I couldn't say anything. Right then, I couldn't open my mouth to say a word.

I was thinking all kinds of things, however: *Oh Lord! What just happened to me? What exactly is going on here? What am I feeling? Is it lust? Is it love? My God! This is the most wonderful feeling in the world. This is the way people are supposed to feel, isn't it?*

At the same time, I was also thinking: *I am married. I have a new baby boy. I'm a Christian, and a Southern Baptist Christian at that. What will people think? Will I perish in hell?*

Like most people in our church, I was raised to believe in a God that got angry at the drop of a hat and punished sinners according to the severity of their sins, and I could not begin to imagine what the punishment would be for something as sinful as what just transpired in my own living room.

I was a complete mess. But in spite of all the troubling feelings in my heart and countless questions whirling in my head, I somehow knew that because of that beautiful solitary kiss, my life would never be the same again.

I came out of my momentary catatonic state and bolted out of Kathleen's lap. I landed on my feet but I can't tell you how. I stood there gaping at her.

Kathleen got up from the chair, walked slowly across the room and out the front door. I didn't stop her from leaving; I couldn't. Later, when we talked about it she said that she was terrified that she had offended me and was worried about what I might do.

After Kathleen left, I dropped back in the chair where she had been sitting and let the lingering warmth of her recent presence encompass me. I don't know how long I sat there and let myself feel over and over again the tenderness of her compelling kiss. I willed myself to recall every single move she had made from the time I opened the door to the time she softly closed the door behind her. I wanted to remember every tiny detail. There was just no way that I would allow myself to forget any part of what had just happened to my body and my heart.

As I sat there, every time a question about my integrity or the wrongness of it all popped into my head, I banished the unwelcome thought. Right then, I did not want to let those guilty ideas get a stranglehold on my mind. I wanted to enjoy the delicious memory and the wonderful sensation of that kiss for as long as I possibly could without having to deal with the obvious implications of what just happened in my living room in my overstuffed green chair.

But the mind does you no favors; it has a predictable way of insisting, of pushing, of forcing you to deeply examine the things in your life that have gradually inched you along to where you are at any particular given moment.

I wondered what in my life had brought me to the point that, although completely surprised, I had allowed a woman to passionately kiss me. It wasn't that I had just permitted it; it was so much more than that. I had actually willingly participated in it and even enjoyed it.

Jesus, who am I kidding? What happened was way beyond just savoring a kiss. Every cell of my being had responded to it; this is who I was meant to be; this is who I really am. What in my past has brought me to this life-changing juncture?

Chapter 2

Mid-1950s

God! Where to start?

Maybe I should start with old Miss Flowers. Yes, she was "Miss" Flowers. That was before the term Ms. was ever thought of. In the mid-1950s, women who were unmarried were called Miss So-and-so, married women were called Mrs. So-and-so, and there was nothing in between. After all, we were women and being married and Mrs. So-and-so was a status. Miss So-and-so said you were on the market and had better get cracking and down that wedding aisle!

Anyway, Miss Flowers was the gym teacher at our local junior high school. It was rumored around Eudora, our small town of about twenty-four thousand in southern Arizona that Miss Flowers and the principal of the school, Miss Euler, were engaged in what my mother, my grandmother and my four aunts called an, "unholy relationship!" I didn't exactly know what an unholy relationship was, but from the tone of their voices I did know that it was something that was just about as bad as it gets.

I was twelve or thirteen at the time, and every time my tribe of female relatives got together for someone's birthday or a holiday they would, as a matter of course, have what they called a "gabfest." They would all sit around the kitchen table and start to wag tongues about everything that was going on in the town and, of course, about all the troubles in the family.

My three sisters and I were all ears. But we especially loved to hear those women get to telling about the awful sins that were going on right under the whole town's noses.

They insisted that something should be done about Miss Flowers. "Just look at her. She dresses just like a man with those black trousers and that white starched short-sleeved shirt and those masculine looking shoes. Doesn't she have any shame at all?" They would ask.

I wondered what they expected a gym teacher to dress like anyhow. I thought she looked okay, except for maybe the weathered brown leather purse she carried over her shoulder all the time. Miss

Flowers had short-clipped graying dark hair, wore thick glasses and had the build of a raw-boned Texas woman.

In a way, I suppose they were right. She did look more than a little on the mannish-side, and that ratty leather purse sure looked as out of place on her as anything I had ever seen.

When all those loud talking, self-righteous kin of mine got started on Miss Flowers and Miss Eller, I tried my best not to miss a single word. I guess you could say that I was intrigued but didn't exactly know why. As I look back on it now, I can't really say that I was any more fascinated about those two women than the rest of my cousins were; all of our ears perked up when we heard their names. We knew the gossip would be juicy and more scandalous than anything else they talked about.

As I was taking it all in I never thought for a half a second that I might eventually be involved in one of those shameful, God forbidden sins that my gossipy female relatives talked about. The way they described it, it sounded like what the revival preachers described as an "abomination to the Lord." For that reason alone, it never occurred to me that I would ever be ensnared in anything as sinful as that.

I wanted to go to heaven when I died; I sure didn't want to perish and burn in everlasting hellfire and damnation. I had burned my hand on the kitchen stove a couple of times, so I could only imagine how terrible and painful being lapped up in flames for eternity would be. To this day, just getting in a hot tub of water reminds me of how hot I thought hell would have been back at that impressionable age.

When there was nothing else to gossip about, they talked about our Pastor Whitfield's wife. Bless her heart. Sister Whitfield played the organ at our Sunday church services. The organ was located on a raised platform where the whole congregation could plainly see Sister Whitfield's legs as she pumped out the hymns on the ancient instrument that had long since seen its better days.

Like most of the other women in the church, Sister Whitfield wore light-colored hose. The only trouble was Sister Whitfield had a massive overgrowth of coarse black curly hair all over her legs. Naturally, when she put on the see-through hose all that black hair got squashed down into what looked like a solid mass of curly ringlets pressed against her legs.

According to all the tongue-waggers in the church, those hose made her legs look like something you'd see on a big old black wooly sheep. Oh my goodness! Even I'll have to admit, those two legs of hers were God-awful ugly, but at the same time it was a funny sight to see.

In our church, it was a sin for women to shave their legs and I guess since Sister Whitfield was the preacher's wife she didn't dare shave hers, even though I'm pretty sure she knew that the church ladies were snickering and talking about her hairy legs behind her back.

There was a lot of preaching in our small Southern Baptist church about going to hell for anything from having your ears pierced to shaving your legs to dancing in the gym during lunch hour at school to divorce to drinking to being unequally yoked together … to name a few! Being unequally yoked together, according to our preacher, meant dating or marrying a Catholic. That was really on the top of the totem pole as far as sins went in our small community — Pretty mild stuff, really, and I was sheltered in many ways by it.

Every so often during a revival, however, a big-time preacher would come to lower the boom on our "backsliding and complacent congregation." The preacher would stomp back and forth, jump up and down on the front pew and preach at the top of his lungs about the upper level of sins … the really terrible ones.

There was a definite hierarchy of sins in these preachers' minds. At the top of the list, there was fornication, adultery, murder and then there was the unmentionable sin, the one that was so bad that it was what the Bible called, "An abomination unto the Lord."

When talking about that one, the preachers got so fired up that the veins would bulge out in their necks, their faces would turn beet red, their eyes would bug out and sweat would pour down their faces. They looked like what I imagined the devil would look like, except of course they didn't have horns or a forked tail or anything.

Those revival ministers sure made a believer out of me though. I sank down in my pew thinking, *never, would I ever be involved in anything that even slightly resembled anything as unholy as what he is preaching about!*

In spite of all those burning in everlasting hell and damnation sermons that I'd heard over the course of my growing up years, there was still something about women having relations with each other that made me more than just a little curious. But, at the time, I didn't have a clue as to why.

I did paid extra attention at school when I was in gym class just to see if I could catch Miss Flowers and Miss Euler engaged in anything that I could report back to my mother, who would immediately pass it along to rest of the hens at their next kitchen table gab party. Unfortunately, I never was able to catch them doing anything other than talking in the hall occasionally. I never even came close to catching them holding hands or, God forbid, kissing, as I imagined people would do if they were involved in one of those "depraved, unholy relationships."

Right away, I guess you can tell that my gaggle of female relatives, those pure-as-the-driven-snow-sinless-saints who spent hours sitting around my mother's kitchen table drinking pot after pot of her coffee, didn't consider themselves polite society. Or, at least, they didn't when they congregated for one of their women's-only gossip sessions.

No, in fact, it was quite the opposite. Anything and anyone was fair game when they got together like that. But even in the heat of a rumor fest, as a general rule they never came right out and said words like "lesbian" or "homosexual"; they referred to the ungodly condition as being "that-a-way."

Ruining someone's reputation over the kitchen table was A-OK for all of them – polite society be damned! My mother was the least gossipmonger of all, but she would join in when the talk really got dirty.

In reflection, the funny thing was that none of them — and I mean not a single one of them — considered gossiping any kind of a sin at all. It wasn't even in the sin category. In their minds, they were just getting together for a little harmless family fun and that was it as far as they were concerned.

Had I known back then that my life would eventually take me to a point that I would be the one that people were watching and whispering about, I can honestly say that I don't know what I would have done. Even as a pre-teen I think I knew deep down inside it was all so hypocritical. But as a young teenager, what can you do about it?

Chapter 3

My sisters and I were well behaved and hardly ever got into any real trouble. Mother believed in a very literal interpretation of the King James Version of the Bible's Book of Proverbs, 13:24 to be exact, where it says, "He who spares his rod hates his son, but he who loves him disciplines him promptly." Anyone who knew our family back then can tell you that my mother was swift to administer the rod.

When my mother, Faith Ann, told us to hop, we asked how high. We didn't give her any backtalk for any reason unless we wanted to be picking ourselves up off the far wall. We were to say "Yes Ma'am" and "No Ma'am" in response to her questions and there were no exceptions.

Once, I made the mistake of answering one of my mother's questions with just a plain ole every day "No." Even though it was a slip of the tongue, it was definitely the wrong reply. Though she always weighed under a hundred pounds unless she was pregnant, that little woman slapped me from the middle of the living room to where I found myself slammed up against the TV set that was back in the corner.

I got the most and worst whippings of her four daughters. Mother used one of my stepfather's old leather belts to beat us with. I can't tell you why to this day, but for the life of me, when I saw her head to the closet for the belt, my little skinny legs started running.

My sister, Midget, would tell me, "Mandy, if you just wouldn't run, she wouldn't whip you so hard." But somehow, I guess, I didn't have enough sense to just stand there and take it like Midget and my younger sisters did. I would run around the house, out in the yard and even scramble under the bed if I could get there before she caught me. I think the faster and longer I ran the madder she got, and that was probably the reason why my whippings were so severe.

The big belt always left ugly, bruised welts on my calves, upper thighs and butt, and there were also times when some of the licks would cut so deep that blood would be running down my legs when she finally wore herself out and finished. Once, the scars had been so noticeable that one of my aunts felt the need to talk with mother about "toning down the punishment just a little." It seemed my aunt feared the church members would start to talk. My mother told my aunt in no uncertain terms to mind her own business and that she would discipline her girls anyway that she saw fit.

Kids played outside back then. We had a TV, but during the day it was mostly the channel pattern, so all the kids in the neighborhood played outdoors for recreation.

My mother would start calling for us to come home when it was time. At first it would be, "Mandy, Midget, Vickie, Nita!" We all had nicknames. If we didn't come right when she called, in about ten minutes or so she would open the front door and holler out our full names, "Amanda Carol Blackwood, Amber Marjorie Blackwood, Alexandra Victoria Hutchison, Anita Julia Haney!" How embarrassing! The whole neighborhood got a good laugh when mother really cut loose like that.

My mother told my sisters and me one by one and as a group that she would kill us if we ever got pregnant out of wedlock. From our past experience with her ironhanded discipline, we believed her to the bone and none of us ever got into any kind of trouble that even resembled something as shameful as that.

I can't imagine what she would have done if one of her daughters had engaged in anything as perverted and forbidden as lesbianism. She probably would have killed us first and then herself. That's how sinful it was thought to be. I'm pretty sure that my mother or any of my aunts ever worried about their girls turning into lesbians. Showing up pregnant was thought to be the worst sin that girls in our community could commit; again, although abused, I was sheltered.

Mother really didn't have to worry about us showing up pregnant; we were died-in-the-wool tomboys and couldn't care less about dressing up in any kind of frilly dress and giggling about boys. Some of our girl cousins, the ones about our same age, were all into boys. So my mother and all the aunts were genuinely fearful that the devil would surely try to entice them away from being virgins.

Having sex and babies out of wedlock was reason enough to be thrown out of the house and disowned by your parents. All the girls in our immediate and extended family never thought of disgracing our families like that. You had to be married to have sex and have kids. That was not only the Southern Baptist Christian way that was the way the entire community believed.

One young girl, a member of our church, was made to walk down to the front and confess her sin of getting pregnant out of wedlock to the congregation. Everyone fell silent as she stood there crying her eyes out and begging them and the Lord above for forgiveness. All the old self-righteous biddies in the church snubbed the poor girl after the Sunday morning she made her confession. I felt so sorry for her I could have cried, but I sure didn't buddy up with her because I knew my mother would beat the holy crap out of me for just speaking to her.

It was crazy how they all acted like they had never done anything wrong. I was pretty sure that some of my aunts and probably most of the other old gossipers in the church weren't as pure as they claimed to be. They most likely had been guilty of at least necking and maybe even slipping into worse sins as they rumbled in the backseats at the drive-in movie before they were married. But they all claimed that they were virgins through and through when they walked down the aisle. I think they lied, but how could you prove it?

Chapter 4

During high school, I worked after school at the local dime store and started thinking about what I wanted to do when I graduated. My stepfather was a real asshole, so I was anxious to get out of the house as soon as I could; but at the time I didn't have any real firm plans in mind.

My stepfather, Ed, was more than just an asshole; he was a sleazebag pervert. I realize those are pretty strong words, but the nasty old creep did some things to my sisters and me that were downright disgusting.

Midget and I were the oldest so we shared a bedroom. Our room was just off the kitchen. It was actually a garage that was haphazardly converted into a bedroom. The door to the room still had a window in it where Ed could push the curtain back to see us changing clothes. He got up early to watch us change from our pajamas into our school clothes. We could see his red, leering face peeking through the glass. That's mortifying for two teenage girls. Even just watching us was violating.

We fixed his wagon though! Midget and I strung up a curtain on our side of the window to prevent him from peeking into our bedroom. My God was he furious when he discovered our handiwork. We heard him stomping away and slamming the pots around in the kitchen outside our door but what could he really say. He would've never admitted that he was wrong in what he was doing.

The bathroom door didn't have a lock, however, and we couldn't keep him from opening the bathroom door on us while we were bathing. Consequently, our baths were as quick as we could possibly make them. We wanted to get in and out before he could open the door and get a smirking look at us. On the weekends when Ed didn't have to work my sisters and I hated to take baths. When it started to get really late and close to our bedtime, Mother would have to threaten us with the belt to make us get in to the bathroom.

Midget and I were constant companions. It was a way of life for us that we tried to protect each other from him. High school girls should never have to protect each other like that.

Ed worked road construction, so when the wind blew the dust and sand so hard that you couldn't see two feet in front of your face he would have to miss work — the whole construction crew shut down. If one of us happened to be home sick when the old weirdo was home for a sandstorm day, he'd creep into our room. He would caress and fondle us while faking concern for our illness. Fortunately, for Midget and me mother was always at home, which prevented him from going any further. My middle sister, Vickie, wasn't as lucky. We learned later after she was grown that he had repeatedly sexually assaulted her; she was in therapy for years.

Of course we told mother, but she just thought he was a sorry SOB. Our mother, like many abused women, thought she had no choice. In her mind, she thought she had no way to raise four girls other than to put up with his physical abuse to her and to us.

I'd seen black eyes and bruises on my mother more times than I could count. Once he threw a Big Ben clock at her. It hit her in the middle of the front of her thigh leaving a huge black bruise in the shape of the clock complete with the ringer on the top.

At the time we girls just thought he was an old mean shit, but once I left home, got away from Eudora and started reading a little, I learned that the deviant acts and the physical abuse he perpetrated on us and our mother could have sent him to prison.

I personally hated his guts and promised myself that when he died that I would attend his funeral so I could do a tap dance on his grave. He was worthless through and through, and it made me wonder if he was part of the reason why I eventually wanted to be with a woman. My only experience with a man growing up was an abusive one, and I saw the way he treated my mother. Some shrinks would probably say "Yes." They would say that those early horrible experiences with him could have contributed to my eventual lesbianism.

While I didn't know anything about being with women when I was younger, I had always thought that I was quite different from the other girls. I just wasn't at all interested in the things that most girls my age were.

I was a tomboy who liked to play ball and do things with my boy cousins. As kids will do, when the boys started going through puberty the first thing they wanted to do was show us their penises, or what our large group of cousins regularly called "wangers."

16

Personally, I thought the whole idea was ridiculous and I honestly had zero interest in what they seemed to be so proud of. I simply wasn't interested in what the opposite sex had to offer at that teen age; it didn't seem that big of a deal back then.

Chapter 5

Late-1950s

When I was just barely seventeen a new guy stationed at the Airbase outside of town started coming to our church. A few months after he started coming, Scott became our choir director. There were many occasions for us to see each other since I sang in the choir and also in the church trio. We didn't see each other alone but just as a matter of course in practicing the church music for Sunday morning services.

Scott was good-looking, outgoing, personable, and everyone at church liked him. He had sandy brown hair, a quick smile and a terrific sense of humor but best of all, he started flirting with me right away. When he could catch my eye while we were practicing the music, he smiled and winked until he finally embarrassed me. His obvious flirting caused me a lot of teasing but I loved it and had no reason to believe that I wasn't meant to be in a heterosexual relationship with a man like Scott.

In fact, I was both flattered and excited that he was interested in me but I really didn't know why he liked me, as there were several really feminine attractive girls going to our small church then. Not that I was ugly or anything. Looking back at my pictures taken at that time I was downright pretty. Not exactly a beautiful swan yet, but the brown freckles that used to cover my face had all but vanished by then, and, with my flashing green eyes and long dark hair, even I could see that I was getting to be more attractive than I used to be.

My tomboy ways hadn't left me, though. I still hated dresses and instead wore jeans, sporty looking tailored slacks and neat cotton blouses whenever I could. Of course it was a sin for girls and women to wear anything other than a dress to church, but even so I did try to keep the lace and frills down to a minimum. In many ways, I was dressing more like Miss Flowers than I realized, although I never connected it and it didn't seem odd to me at the time.

My cousin, Loraine, was one of the frilly girly-girls. Her mother, Aunt Georgia, was jealous that Scott was paying attention to me instead of her precious daughter; maybe that is why I was so excited Scott took a fancy to me. My mother liked Scott too, but was very nervous about my dating him as he was already twenty and she thought he was way too old for me.

Now that I'm thinking about Loraine, there is something that happened with her that might have some real bearing on this subject. When I was younger, Loraine had what I thought at the time were strange inclinations toward me. Every now and then I spent the night at her house. I didn't spend the night to visit with Loraine; I spent the night to play with my male cousins. But since I was a girl I slept in the same double bed with Loraine. It wouldn't have been right and decent for me to bunk in with the boys.

After all the lights went out in the house and without saying a word, Loraine would start rubbing my upper arm and my shoulder. Then later on when I didn't object, she got a little bolder and started caressing my thigh, the thigh that was next to her. That was as far as it went. I liked it but also thought it was a little on the weird side. Loraine never pursued her lesbian tendency and went on to marry a guy that owned a Texas auction house. But, maybe it wasn't Miss Flowers and Miss Euler after all; maybe it was Loraine that first aroused those forbidden feelings in me.

But Scott liked me and not Loraine and as you can imagine, I got the old pregnancy lecture from my mother on a regular basis. Scott and I could go out on Friday and Saturday nights but I had to be in the house by 10 p.m. sharp. If I didn't come in the house by 10 on the dot my mother would flick the porch light off and on as a signal for me to come in the house immediately. Flicking the lights off and on was the standard way that parents got their dating teenage daughters to come in the house on time.

It was a little embarrassing but Scott took it pretty good-naturedly. "I think your Mama wants you to come on in," he would tease. Knowing there would be at least some hard stares when I got in the house, even if I were only one minute late past 10 p.m., I would go on in just to prevent a devil of a scene.

There wasn't all that much for us to do in Eudora except go to the movies, listen to music on the radio, have a hamburger at the drive-in or go visit some married friends of Scott's and play cards. Every now and then just for a little change up, we would go out in the desert and chase jackrabbits by the light of the moon in Scott's bright red Chevy pickup truck. Like I said, there wasn't a whole lot to do in Eudora.

We dated for a few months and then Scott asked me to marry him. I was flattered and I really thought I was in love with him, but for Christ's sake who knows anything about being in love when they are seventeen years old? I didn't know anything; I was a baby. But it was accepted and even expected that most girls would get married when they got out of high school so there wasn't an objection from either Scott's parents or mine.

Scott's dad, Brother Allen, who was a Southern Baptist preacher back in Paducah, Kentucky, drove all the way out to Eudora with his hypochondriac wife, Polly, in the seat beside him. I swear to God, that man had to be a saint in the making. Polly would have driven Jesus to drink. For positive certain, I know that poor man was glad when that sixteen hundred mile trip was over.

Scott's mother was a nonstop complainer; if she was awake, she was griping about something. She was one of those women who got the "vapors" at the drop of a hat. She drove me insane from the get-go and I had to make myself be around her for Scott and Brother Allen's sake.

Her many prolonged pseudo illnesses had been the reason that Scott and his brother were sent off to a boarding school when they were both ten years old. They practically grew up at the school and, in my opinion, I think they both suffered lasting emotional damage. I know Scott did. He craved a home of his own and he did not want to share it with anyone, including kids. Even though he felt that way he didn't bother to share that important bit of information with me. I had to find it out for myself the hard way a number of years later.

We had a wedding at our small church in Eudora. Scott's dad officiated and then he and Polly climbed back in their old four-door grocery-getter-green Oldsmobile and headed back to Kentucky. Scott and I got a tiny one-bedroom apartment over someone's garage in Eudora. I finished up high school and then Scott got orders to transfer to Montgomery, Alabama.

Chapter 6

I was thrilled to be traveling so far away from our small desert town. The only reason people lived there was the Airbase. The sand that shut down Ed's construction work blew there like something out of a science fiction movie, and living with the sandstorms was a nightmare for everyone. We walked to school and when the sandstorms hit we would take a few steps and then squat down on our legs to keep the sand from biting into the tender skin on the backs of them.

When there was word of a dirt or sandstorm coming, the wives would run out and gather their clothes off the line to keep them from looking like pure mud. At our house after a sandstorm we had to literally shovel the dirt out of the doorways and rake it off the windowsills. My mother had severe allergies, so Midget and I were the ones to clean the house after the frequent storms. We hated them and that was one of the major reasons why I was so happy to leave the place behind me. Oh I cried a little leaving my mother and sisters, but the tears didn't last long. In fact, I think they had pretty much dried up by time we hit the city limits out of Eudora.

Scott and I never did have much in the passion department but I don't think that either of us knew any better. I know I didn't. Tell me, if you've never had an orgasm how would you know what you were missing?

But we were terrific friends and really genuinely enjoyed each other's company; this was the foundation of our relationship, which seemed normal to me and so much better than what my mother and Ed had. We went fishing, played cards with friends, had cookouts and went to church and local ballgames, just the stuff regular people do. Honestly, I didn't know what I was going without in the romance department. We were good to each other and I thought that was just the way life was supposed to be. I considered myself lucky and thought I was in love.

We liked it in Montgomery, but as I had never been around any black people it took me a while to get used to the whole idea of racism, which was rampant there. At that time, it seemed like everything was about segregation and the differences between the blacks and the whites. We did have lots of Mexicans where I came from but there wasn't all that hate going on; we co-existed and got along, accepting and understanding each other's culture and differences.

I was getting bored out of my mind with nothing to do all day except clean house and cook dinner; I wanted to make something out of myself besides being just a housewife. I went to Drones Business College, took secretarial classes and learned how to take shorthand and type so I could get a job to bring in some extra money. Before I could actually get a job though, Scott got transferred again back to his hometown in Paducah as a recruiter for the Air Force.

That's where I got my first real office job working for a mean, older-than-dirt southern lawyer. His long-drawl of a southern accent was so thick that I had to get the other secretaries on the floor to come listen to his dictation so I could type his Warranty Deeds. It sounded like he had a mouthful of marbles!

His office was on the second floor of a building with no elevator. The whole floor knew when he was coming up the stairs because we could hear his loud grunts as he took each step up to our floor. He should have retired his old, cranky self ten years before that, but everyone in town knew him for Deed work and he just kept doing Warranty Deeds until the day he keeled over.

He was really set in his ways and hard to work for but I toughed it out. He was the most forgetful person I'd ever known. When he left his battered, worn out briefcase somewhere he would inevitably accuse me of misplacing it. Many days I felt like crying and giving up; he was abusive like my stepfather, but I kept at it because I didn't want to let Scott or myself down. I was determined to make this work not only for the extra income but to prove to myself that I was more than what my mother and Ed had beaten me into believing; that I was worth something; that I could be successful at what I set my mind to do ... that I could support myself and be independent if I needed to be.

One thing that really ticked me off about him was he insisted on calling me by my legal name; it had to be Amanda and never Mandy for him. Why, I will never know. Maybe it was only to irritate me or maybe, in his mind, he just had to have everything legal and proper.

I did learn from the other secretaries that I was the thirteenth secretary the old attorney had had in the three months prior to my getting the job. All the other secretaries on the floor were all taking bets to see how long I would last. That only made me more determined to stay and make it work.

We attended the same church where Scott's dad was the preacher. As I had learned when I first met him, Brother Allen was a mild-mannered sort of guy so he didn't really preach about going to hell all that much. Nevertheless, the atmosphere in the church was pretty much the same as it had been in the church where I grew up; you could describe it as one of those God-fearing churches where pretty much everything was a sin – including shaving your legs.

Since I was the minister's daughter-in-law I was sure that there was an entire church full of self-righteous old, busybody vultures ready to pounce on me or anybody else that dared to stray from the fold even in the least little bit. The memories of my mother and her sisters sitting around the kitchen table gossiping haunted me; I just knew women in my church were doing the same thing and I was the topic of their mean-spirited gossip.

What was worse was there were still the visiting hellfire and brimstone revival preachers that would preach to high heaven about how loathsome it was to be involved in homosexuality. Sometimes, when they would preach like that, there was a little twinge of guilt in me but I didn't understand why; I was – what I thought – happily married in a heterosexual relationship. I had no reason to feel guilty about homosexuality.

Chapter 7

Like most young married women I wanted to have a baby after a few years but Scott was unenthusiastic about the idea. He still didn't outright tell me that he was against having kids but he was more than just a little half-hearted about us trying to get pregnant. There was something not quite right about the way he was acting but I pushed for children anyway.

At the time I had never connected his childhood and selfishness, the outright obsession of being the only one and having his own space without having to share with anyone, including a child; I simply didn't realize that he was so adamant about not adding to our family, and he never told me directly his innermost feelings about the subject. So I moved forward planning a family, and after failing to conceive the old-fashioned way I went to several different specialists; I even went to Louisville to see the best fertility doctors in the state.

I did everything the specialists asked me to do, but after a year or so of doing what they told me the last specialist finally confirmed, "You need to adopt; you will never be able to get pregnant."

Suddenly, Scott and I were arguing about adopting a lot. Both our parents and all of our friends thought it would be a terrific idea. Of course the church family thought it would be wonderful too, but I suppose Scott thought as long as I couldn't get pregnant he wouldn't have to face his fear of having a baby, much less be honest with me about how against the idea he really was. He thought he was home clean – no pregnancy, no baby.

I persisted though; I wanted to be a mom. This was another fulfilling way to prove to myself that I was better than what I was raised to believe. I was good worker, a good wife and I wanted to be a good mom. I don't know why, but finally after a lot of talk and many arguments Scott agreed to go though the state adoption application process. I was elated. I was finally getting my baby; I couldn't have been happier.

Within a short six months, we passed all the application red tape with flying colors and were on the waiting list for getting a baby. Six weeks after we got on the waiting list they called to say they had a baby boy for us.

I, of course, was thrilled out of my mind; Scott was quiet and even sullen on the way to pick up our six-week-old son. The social worker noticed Scott's less than enthusiastic behavior and asked him if he was sure about the adoption. Scott said that he was fine with it and I guess she chalked up his strange behavior to being a nervous new father – so did I to be completely honest.

Before we picked him up, we had already named our little baby boy Patrick. With his sandy reddish hair, little fat yet muscular legs and bright blue eyes, I thought he was the most beautiful baby in the world. Even though he was wearing a tiny blue knit cap and was tightly wrapped up in a light blue receiving blanket, I could tell that he was going to be an athlete right from the first second I saw him.

From the moment we got in the car with our precious son Scott refused to touch him or even look at him. He looked straight ahead for the entire two hours that it took for us to drive back to Paducah. There was no conversation. I was shocked; it seemed like he was shunning us but I couldn't comprehend why as I held this amazing creature in my arms. How could anyone, much less the adoptive father resist loving this beautiful miracle. I believe God had given me Patrick. He had heard my prayers and blessed me with my son when I couldn't conceive my own. I believe God wanted me to have Patrick, and he wanted Scott to have him too. I couldn't understand Scott's behavior and rejection of this blessing, this miracle of God. It seemed blasphemous in my eyes … and we weren't even home yet.

Scott's parents and some of our friends were waiting for us at home. They were all so wildly ecstatic about our new little boy that I don't think they even noticed the immediate 180-degree change in Scott. If anyone did, they were probably thinking like the social worker and imagined he was worrying about his new fatherly responsibilities.

I tried to talk to Scott as soon as everyone left but he refused to talk to me or to look at me or to let me touch him … and that was that. Within less than one day, one 24-hour period, my husband began to reject me and our newly adopted baby. That's how our life went for six months after we got little baby Patrick. We lived in the same house, we slept in the same bed, but there was only minimal communication and zero physical contact with either Patrick or me. Scott wouldn't even walk into Patrick's room.

The responsibility for taking care of the baby was 100 percent mine and I was okay with that. From the first moment I held Patrick in my arms he was my son. Instantly, in my heart and in my mind I took on the responsibility of being his mother and I never looked back. Regardless of how Scott behaved I knew that I could not and would not let this little angel down. Yes, of course, I hoped that Scott would warm up to Patrick over time. I wanted my best friend and my happy marriage back. But if Scott didn't come around, I would still do everything in my power to give Patrick the love and life he deserved. My priorities had changed from being a wife to being a mother; my priorities had changed at the hand of my husband.

During those bizarre six months I felt abandoned and I really didn't know which way to turn. I didn't want to admit to our friends and families how bad things really were because I hoped Scott would change his mind over time. I couldn't admit how bad things were because I couldn't give the church gossipmongers something to talk about. What would they say if they knew that the preacher's son and choir director took his wife to adopt a baby and never spoke to them again once the transaction was complete? What could they say? They would blame me; somehow, I just knew they would blame me.

Although he didn't say so, Scott was punishing me for getting Patrick. Scott was gone every day and every night doing something; he deliberately made plans to be gone. It was so different than our life had been before when we had done everything together.

Patrick and I had each other but I still felt isolated, left out of things and rejected by my husband. It seemed that my pushing for Patrick had destroyed our marriage and our home.

At first I cried a lot, but then as time went on I realized that Scott was the one at fault. I was his wife, his companion, yet he never truthfully shared with me his absolute commitment to not having children. He never told me point blank, "I don't want children, Mandy, and I will reject any child you bring into this house." We fought about it but he was never honest with me about how serious this was to him and I felt betrayed.

Here I was a single mother with a husband still who expected us to keep up our image in town. I often wondered if that is why he agreed to adopt Patrick in the first place, peer pressure to keep the image of the perfect Southern Baptist family. If they only knew what was happening behind closed doors.

Beginning to sense something was wrong, Scott's mother and some our friends tried to talk to Scott but it did absolutely no good. Even Brother Allen tried to talk to him and Scott told him to butt out. Of course, he didn't use those exact words with his dad but Brother Allen got the message loud and clear. Scott wouldn't listen to anyone. The baby and his behavior toward us was a dead subject as far as Scott was concerned. He was the head of the household and that was that.

Since Scott was the choir director we continued to go to church together and played the roles of the happy, young couple. I was still the leader of the Young People's Department. Our appearances at church were just to keep the church community and Scott's parents from knowing the real depth of the difficulties in our relationship.

By this time, just being in the car with him for the trip back and forth to church was a huge struggle. He had made it plainly clear that he wanted nothing to do with Patrick or me. We simply went to church and he drove us back home where he dropped Patrick and me off and then went on to play golf or go fishing or hunting or something. There was always something. It irked him to be at home with Patrick and me, even for a few minutes.

After months of his dismissal of us, I was beginning to realize that my initial dream of Scott changing his mind was just that, a fantasy. I started to accept the truth that things would never be the same again. Looking back, it was more than just that — there was a definite shift occurring in me. Scott had hurt me more than I'd ever thought it possible for any human to hurt me. I'd been abused, beaten and sexually assaulted, yet this hurt more.

I was beginning to realize that my feelings for Scott were gradually changing, and not for the better either, despite my efforts to make my marriage and our parenthood work. In time, I didn't care so much if he wasn't home. Him being home caused undue stress and discomfort for both Patrick and me, and I started to see us eventually living our lives without Scott.

Chapter 8

Kathleen was what was called a "nontraditional student" and was finishing up her graduate work at Murray State University, which was about an hour's drive from Paducah. She was really gifted in math and wanted a career using her mathematics degree.

Her father, John Crutchfield, practically owned a small farming town just a few miles from Paducah. The Crutchfields owned the feed store, the grocery store, the gas station, the farm equipment store and ran a huge farm too. Kathleen was the oldest of five kids and she helped her dad with all the bookkeeping and the running of the stores. She had an apartment in Murray, but came home on Wednesdays and every weekend so she could be as much help as possible. The whole family including her mother, Mary, worked really hard every day except Sunday; they had to with as much as they owned.

From the moment I first met her, there had always been something strangely unusual about Kathleen. Maybe it was the way she looked at me sometimes over the upright piano that was in our Young Peoples Department, or maybe it was the way she would help me out to the car with Patrick after church on Sundays. Even now I still can't put my finger on it, but there was something that made her special. She had an easy way about her, but she also knew what she wanted out of life. There was no doubt in her mind that she would be very successful.

She made it obvious that she liked both Patrick and me, and she really didn't have a problem interacting with Scott in a friendly yet impersonal sort of way. There were plenty of guys that came into her father's stores that were like Scott, so she was used to putting up with their charm and banter in their attempts to date the well-to-do John Crutchfield's daughter.

Obviously I learned later that she wouldn't give two cents for most men, but she would put up a good front to keep old John's customers happy. John wanted her to hurry up and get finished with school, come back home for good, get married and "have me some grandbabies," as he put it. Mr. Crutchfield wanted her to marry one of the local boys, one who would inherit one of the other big farms in the area, but of course he didn't have an inkling of what Kathleen had going on in her head. No one did.

John had no idea that Kathleen planned to move as far away from her hometown and her family as possible. She liked kids, but never planned to have any of her own. According to her, as the oldest she had already had her fill of changing diapers, wiping noses and raising kids. She'd paid her dues and it was time for her to be selfish.

Kathleen and I got to be good friends at church and would see each other at the different church functions; I knew that I really liked her. I was so hurt and lonely from the way Scott had been treating me since we adopted Patrick that I guess I was starved for any kind of attention, but it never occurred to me that there was anything going on except a really good friendship until the day she kissed me when she came by my house on her way back from college that Friday afternoon.

The tender kiss revealed more than Kathleen's intentions in our "friendship." It left me to ponder the first two decades of my entire life; to wonder why and how I ended up at this point in my life; to relive all the pain and happiness from my childhood, teenage and young adult years.

After reviewing my life like I had, while there were a few things in my past that some would say contributed to my propensity toward lesbianism, I still don't think anything in my youth was it. I believe it was Kathleen and her kiss. I still don't know exactly what made me so receptive to her compelling kiss other than, obviously, it was my destiny, but that Friday afternoon changed my and Patrick's life forever.

Chapter 9

Early 1960s

That beautiful life-changing kiss was on a Friday afternoon; I wouldn't see Kathleen again until Sunday at church. I couldn't wait for Saturday to crawl by, to waste by; I desperately wanted to see her again. I didn't know what I would say to her, I was just sick to see her and that is the only way to describe it.

When Sunday morning finally came I walked into my Young People's Department early and Kathleen was already waiting for me there in the empty room. She didn't have to ask and I didn't have to say. We instantly understood that the magic between us the previous Friday was mutual. We didn't touch each other; without talking about it, we already knew better than to do that. Our eyes merely told each other what we'd both been dying to say: *It's okay.*

As people began to fill the classroom I was amazed that they didn't detect the tension in the air between Kathleen and me. That was the first of literally hundreds of times that I breathed a quiet sigh of relief knowing that our secret had not been discovered.

After class I asked Kathleen to come over to my house that afternoon as Scott was going to play golf. At my invitation she gave a happy wink of approval, her gorgeous full lips turned up into the biggest smile I'd ever seen. She didn't walk but bounced along the sidewalk as she helped Patrick and me out to the car.

When she came over to my house after church, I can tell you right to this day what she was wearing: a pair of brown slacks, a white polo style shirt and some of those brown loafers with the tassels on the toe. Kathleen was like me, a neat sporty dresser. I guess you could say that we were both androgynous looking. She had long sandy blond hair and we were both athletic and about the same size, about five-foot-five.

At last at my house when were finally alone there was the same long passionate stare that I had seen the past Friday. But this time, emboldened by my feelings for her, my eyes brazenly returned her intense gaze.

I was thinking, *Amazing, this is simply amazing! How have Kathleen and I, the most implausible of people, discovered that unique something that makes people change the entire direction of their lives? Or in my case, what has in an instant changed my sexual orientation? Has it been there all along and I just haven't been aware of it?*

I didn't care. Kathleen was beautiful that day and our passionate gaze said it all. She didn't have to worry about whether she was offending me this time; we both knew that we were already past that point.

Chapter 10

Since her father was a deacon in our church, my father-in-law was the preacher and my husband was the choir director, we had to watch every move we made. The brief periods that we spent together were planned so as not to raise suspicion from any quarter.

Kathleen didn't want to hurt her family; really she thought that it would destroy her dad if he found out. I didn't want to hurt anyone either. Plus, I didn't want anyone to find out because Patrick's adoption wouldn't be final for another a year and a half and I was scared that he would be taken from me. For all of those reasons and more, Kathleen and I lived double lives in every respect. No one could ever know our secret.

On some weekends, I took Patrick to spend the weekend at Kathleen's apartment near her college. There in that tiny apartment for those forty-eight hours we were free to be ourselves. Those few unforgettable nights we spent together were what kept us believing that we could continue the charade until enough time had passed that Patrick's adoption was final.

We played with Patrick until it was his bedtime. Then we had candle-lit dinners on her small living room floor. We danced and we made hungry, unbridled love. Just to be in the same room together was happiness for us.

Learning how to make love to her was easy; she was a qualified teacher and I learned from her exactly what to do.

She kissed my lips, my mouth, my breasts and slowly, ever so slowly, moved her hands and lips down the middle of my stomach. Then, even more slowly, she moved teasingly past my stomach. "Kathleen," I whispered as she expertly began to gently massage between my legs. I felt myself getting moist. She was barely stroking me with her fingertips at first and then her lovely mouth was finding its way to my warm wet secret place. Her lips and mouth were soft and gentle at first, but the rhythm became increasingly more demanding. I could feel the very deepest parts of my body responding to her rhythmic in and out strokes.

Kathleen's undulating rhythm soon took a magical possession of me. It moved and danced and gradually awakened a long denied yearning, a yearning that was suddenly alive with desire.

Matching her rhythm, my body forcefully answered her pulsating cadence. And then, abruptly, my body held itself taut. I didn't move; I didn't need to move; I didn't want to move. I remember thinking, *don't let this end*, and then there was a moment of no thought; no thought at all. But by then it was too late, some slight shift, just a tiny caress caused the eruption of ecstasy. It washed over me. Every cell of my body was awake, alive, ignited and for a few exquisite moments I thought, *this is as close to heaven as I will ever be*. It didn't take long; I had unknowingly been waiting for this incomparable stunning moment all my life.

Yes, I experienced my first orgasm with Kathleen. It was perfect! It was out of this world! How do you describe something so glorious? Of course, I wanted it to last forever. Afterward, we held each other and cried together from the sheer joy of the moment.

Then, we lay in each other's arms but not for long. It was my turn and I had learned well. My beautiful Kathleen loved me, trusted me to bring her the gift of explosive orgasms and I did; we did. We were happy. We were passionately in love.

With no doubt we knew we had to be extremely careful but we knew whatever we had to do to see and be with each other would be worth it. We had found something that few people ever find and we made a promise to each other that we would make our impossible situation work somehow.

Chapter 11

Kathleen and I were honest, open people. Sneaking around like we were was difficult for both of us. Kathleen was better at thinking on her feet than I was, but we were both inexperienced at acting like nothing was different between us. From the moment I saw her that Sunday morning after our first kiss we were both on high alert. We had to be.

Isn't it strange when you have nothing to hide you can automatically act naturally? Even something that might appear very suspicious when you are innocent can be explained away with wide-eyed blamelessness? But when you are deliberately trying to hide something, any little thing out of the ordinary can make you worry about how it will look and how you are going to fabricate something halfway believable? We were reacting with guilty consciences.

Ordinary everyday life was different. Our loved ones became potential enemies. Given their religious beliefs even they would not hesitate to destroy our relationship if they found out about it.

We had a plan to carry us through until Kathleen finished school and until Patrick's adoption was final. We would move away with Patrick to a large city and just be absorbed into the population. We wouldn't stand out like sore thumbs like we would if we stayed in Paducah. Our plan was to see each other when we could and play our separate parts until moving time.

I had to pretend to the church people and to Scott's mom and dad that I was still interested in my marriage, which I had grown out of. I attended holiday events with Scott over at his parents' house and continued my position at church as the Youth leader. I had to keep up the façade that we were a happy family, even though Scott was still staying away from home and treating both Patrick and me like we didn't exist so. Admittedly, I was thankful that I didn't have to actually deal with him most of the time; it made surviving this period of my life easier.

Kathleen had to act as if nothing was different in her life, either. She had to continue in her dad's businesses, continue driving back and forth to school, keep up with her classes and feign interest in the young, male suitors that solicited her father's stores so she could get married and have those grandbabies.

Kathleen and I both hated it when I had to get in the car with Scott to go home after church. We couldn't wait for her to go home and eat Sunday dinner with her family and then drive the few miles to my house so we could be together for just a few hours; she would leave from my house to head back to the university. We were very cautious when we were together; we didn't allow ourselves to get into any compromising situations.

There were a few close calls, like the time Scott came home from playing golf early one Friday afternoon when Kathleen had dropped by. Scott got sick with a case of diarrhea on the golf course and had to leave at the tenth hole. Kathleen and I weren't really doing anything except talking, but we both jumped like we'd been shot when we heard his truck in the driveway.

When Scott came in he hustled right past us and went straight to the bathroom. I think he was embarrassed that he had shit his pants on the golf course and he didn't want Kathleen's dad to hear of his unfortunate "explosion." After all, he had a reputation to maintain and even something as innocent as an unforeseen sickness can get blown out of proportion in a small town.

There was another time when Scott's nosy mom stopped by with no warning. This time, when Polly knocked on the door Kathleen and I hadn't even heard her car. She was already at the front door and ringing the doorbell before we knew anyone was anywhere around. Customarily, she rang the bell once and then barged on in. Thank God, we had the door locked on this occasion or she would have seen Kathleen and me necking on the sofa like no tomorrow. We didn't have a clue that anyone was even in the county, much less right there on the front porch. After months of "living the lie," as we called it, we were both exhausted.

By this time Scott had started to see the error of his ways and now, all of a sudden, he wanted his family back. He apologized over and over for treating Patrick and me as if we didn't exist. He even wanted us to be intimate again. I was more stunned at this turn of behavior than I was at his initial behavioral switch. I found myself incredulously wondering, *how do you totally ignore your baby and your wife for this many months and then just want to take up where you left off?* That just wasn't going to happen, not ever. I was stronger than this. I was not my mother and I did not want to stay in an abusive relationship.

I could not bear to be in the same room with him anymore, much less actually consider having sex with him. I understood what lovemaking was supposed to be like now and it certainly wasn't his brand of inept hop-on-and-off sex. I wondered how long I could put off his pawing me.

I also understood what tenderness and love were. What true love was; not a façade to keep your family, friends, church and community in the dark as to how you really treat your wife and son. I understood companionship with someone who actually wanted to be my partner, my lover, not someone who considered me a token, and I wanted to continue in my partnership with Kathleen because I loved her and she loved me; she truly cared about me and my son.

Unfortunately, I had to make Scott believe that there was a chance for us, when at the same time I knew that no chance in hell that I would ever really be with him again. I knew that I had to keep Scott's and my marriage together at least on the surface just long enough for Patrick's adoption to be final.

I was torn. My upbringing was catching up with me and tearing me apart. Everything I was told was wrong felt right, and everything I was told was right felt wrong. I was in love with a woman and my husband was a man. What was worse, he was a man that I no longer loved or respected. I didn't know what I was going to do and the tension slowly gnawed away at my ability to hang on.

I knew if Kathleen and I allowed our minds to run wild, there were a million things that could go wrong to give us away. If we made just one tiny slip we would be exposed, and I became obsessed with finding us a way out.

One day as I was worrying myself into the next world over what to do, Scott walked in and startled me. I honestly couldn't take it anymore – his treatment, the emotional and mind games he played on me, the lie I was living – and before I knew it I blurted out, "Scott we need to talk."

Mandy Episode 2

Chapter 1

Franklin D. Roosevelt said, " … the only thing we have to fear is fear itself — nameless, unreasoning, unjustified terror?" The quote meant little to me when I studied our nation's history, but now the overwhelming truth of his words continually haunted me.

Nothing had really happened to make me feel this way; nevertheless, a paralyzing dread permeated the hours, minutes, and even the seconds of my days. In fact, during the last few weeks, the sense of impending doom had escalated to the point that I didn't see how I could continue to live as I was living for even a little while longer; yet, I knew that I absolutely had to.

I realized, of course, that under the circumstances, several different distressing possibilities were on the table, but the thing I feared the most was the likelihood that this volatile situation would cause me to lose my precious baby boy.

The rest of it I could deal with over time, like losing my home, my income, and my stature in the community. But knowing myself like I did, I knew in my heart that if I lost Patrick, the knowledge that my relationship with Kathleen had caused it would haunt me for the rest of my life. Whatever I had to do, I could not let that happen.

Scott Allen, my husband, silently wolfed down the dinners I made so he could hurry and get out of the house every night. Hunkering down over his food, his elbows and forearms surrounded his plate so he could shovel it in more quickly. He usually had his entire supper eaten within less than three minutes. Under different circumstances, the way he was acting would have been funny. It had become so ridiculous that I sometimes wondered if he had a stopwatch in his pocket and was trying to beat his time from the previous evening.

As soon as he finished his meal, he pushed his chair away from the table so hard that it screeched and left deep scuffs on my newly waxed hardwood dining room floor. Then he grabbed his jacket off the coat rack in the hall and, without a word, stomped across the room and slammed the door behind him. From the manner of his exit, you would have thought we just had a big fight or something, but, no, we never argued at all; instead, suffocating silence characterized our existence.

Whatever was going on with Scott it sure wasn't affecting his appetite, but that wasn't true for me. When I am upset, my appetite flies out the window and making myself eat becomes a real chore. Typically, after Scott banged out the door, I just sat and stared at my plate. I would eventually make myself eat a few bites, knowing that I had to keep my strength up in order to take care of little Patrick.

Before all of this started I could go to sleep as soon as my head hit the pillow; now the nights were a seemingly endless wrestling match between the cotton sheets, the comforter, and me. Makeup helped, but didn't really hide the dark circles that had started to appear under my eyes. Store clerks and the church folks frequently asked me if I was all right.

Terrified that my husband, our families, and also our small Southern Baptist community would somehow discover my forbidden secret, my life, except for Kathleen and Patrick, had in many ways deteriorated into a living hell.

Just driving to the grocery store in our baby blue 1964 Thunderbird convertible made me jumpy. Everyone knew the car, and I imagined that every old busybody gossip in town was watching me. In my mind, they were ready to pounce on me at my slightest mistake. From my strict Southern Baptist upbringing, I knew all too well about how people gossiped about the minister's family.

I was walking a tight rope between two opposing worlds. On the one hand, I was a high-profile member of a small Southern Baptist community; on the other hand, I was deeply involved in what my family and my church thought was one of the worst sins that Satin could ever tempt a person with — it was right up there with murder and child molestation as far as the hierarchy of sins in our church were concerned.

The hard truth was that if the church members somehow got wind of who I really was and what I had been doing, it would be the biggest scandal that had ever hit our little, mostly Southern Baptist community.

People thought the preacher's family should set a good example for the congregation and also the people who lived in town.

They were to live sinless lives as much as possible, and if they ever did sin, it sure better be one of the minor sins like telling a little white lie or getting your ears pierced.

Should my secret come to light, I would be shunned right out of town and all the rest of my family would be ridiculed and made fun of, too. The gossipmongers would have a field day, that much I knew for sure. Living through their finger-pointing and contemptuous laughter wouldn't be pleasant; however, losing Patrick would be unbearable.

Chapter 2

God help me, it was true. I, Mandy Allen, the wife of the preacher's son, was desperately in love with a graduate student, Kathleen Crutchfield, a beautiful, kind, smart, educated woman. But I was married to a man whom I no longer loved. In fact, I truly loathed Scott, and with good reason, too.

From the instant the social worker put little six-week-old Patrick in my arms, Scott had made it his primary purpose in life to ignore both the baby and me. He came, went, and acted as if Patrick and I were not even in the house. To him, we might as well have been old, used newspapers piled up in the corner waiting for the trash.

Scott and I had been best friends and constant companions the seven years before we went to pick up our baby at the state adoption agency. Like night and day, the change in Scott had been instant. One second he was my friend and husband; the next he was a total stranger. A side of him I'd never known showed up the day we got Patrick. My mind just couldn't wrap itself around the drastic difference in Scott. What should have been the happiest day of our lives turned into a nightmare and the beginning of the end of our marriage.

During the first few weeks after we got our little cotton-topped, blue-eyed angel, I'd hoped, given enough time, that Scott would go back to being the warm, fun-loving man I'd married and had been sharing my life with. But day after day came and went, with Scott giving both the baby and me the proverbial brush off, the cold, silent treatment. He never actually looked at either one of us; he looked through us like we were invisible to him.

Scott refused to talk to me about anything, period. Conversation between us wasn't strained; it didn't exist. We carried on the business of the household like two zombies. When the tension would get so bad that I thought I might explode, I'd try to ask him why he was ignoring the baby and me. He always walked past me and out the door like he hadn't heard a word I'd said. This was how our life went for months.

Chapter 3

Though I did have a strong suspicion, I didn't, for a fact, exactly know what was going on with Scott. He had changed on a dime from someone who had loved and protected me to someone who I felt actually hated Patrick and me.

It mirrored the way my abusive stepfather acted toward my sisters and me when we were growing up. Insanely jealous of our mother, our stepfather, Ed, couldn't stand the thought of her having been married to other men before him. Ed despised even the sight of us, because we looked so much like our respective fathers. Mother had been married twice before, and Ed knew that before they got married.

For no apparent reason, he would get mad at us and yell at Faith Ann, our mother, about what a burden we were and how glad he would be to get rid of us. He constantly complained about how much it cost to put a roof over our heads and how much he spent trying to feed us.

All the food was rationed the entire time we lived with him, except when it came to Anita, his daughter and the baby of the family. Anita could have a whole quart of milk if she wanted it, but we could only have half a glass, and that was if we were lucky. Ed kept track of everything we ate down to the last pinto bean. It was a horrible way to live, but when you are in the midst of something like that as a child, what can you really do?

Poor mother dreaded it when one of us got sick enough to have to see old Doctor Bennett. Mainly, it was because she would have to listen to Ed rant on and on about how much the doctor's visit had set him back.

One year when I was eleven, I became violently ill with a continuous headache, sky rocketing fever, and horrific vomiting that wouldn't stop. After three days of this, my mother finally threw such a fit that Ed allowed her to take me to see the doctor. I was immediately admitted to the hospital for tests.

The spinal tap revealed that I had polio. They didn't have the Salk vaccine yet, so I was rushed by ambulance to the state isolation hospital in Phoenix. There were iron lungs in the rooms and even out in the halls. There had been a polio epidemic in our state and in the neighboring states of New Mexico and California. As an eleven-year-old child, hearing all the strange sounds the machines made as they breathed for other young polio victims was terrifying. All polio patients had to be quarantined, so I had to stay in the hospital by myself for two weeks.

My mother and my sisters followed the ambulance all the way from Eudora to Phoenix, but after I was admitted to the hospital, all they could do was see me through the window of my second story hospital room. They had to leave me there, and even though I was as sick as a dog, one of the nurses helped me to the window so I could get a last glimpse of my family when they were leaving to go back to Eudora. I remember them all waving to me, getting in the car, and pulling out of the hospital parking lot. I was luckier than most of the other kids, I only ended up with a curvature of the spine that was eventually fixed through physical therapy.

Ed was furious over what he imagined the hospital costs would be, but before mother had married Ed, she had, for some unknown reason, purchased a little specialty insurance policy from one of those traveling insurance salesman; luckily, it covered polio. Amazingly, all the bills were paid by that dinky, inexpensive policy.

They had horrible arguments where Ed ended up beating my ninety-seven pound mother and all of us girls along with her. Afraid for our mother, us three older girls would jump into the fray. It was commonplace for him to knock our little, skinny bodies up against the wall as fast as we got within arm's length of him. Their fights were always a free-for-all, but inevitably, Ed would beat the hell out of all of us before it was all through.

Once, my middle sister, Vickie, actually got the best of Ed. All of us girls were sitting in a line on the sofa and, suddenly, he came at Vickie, intent on slapping her across her face. As soon as he got within range, Vickie, instinctively, and without really aiming, kicked him in the privates hard enough to make him yelp, clutch himself, whimper, and hobble as fast as he could out of the room.

I suppose Vickie had really hurt him, because we didn't see any more of him the rest of that night. Later, he told our mother that he would kill the next one of us that ever kicked him in the privates again. We still laugh about Vickie's accidental, but well-placed, blow to this day.

One of the reasons that I married Scott was because he seemed so different than my mean, crazy stepfather. Scott was easygoing and had a great sense of humor. We had always gotten along during the seven years we had been married. There were certainly never any physical fights or even a hint that there ever would be.

Oh, we argued every now and then like other couples did, but we settled our disagreements usually within an hour or two. We had a standing agreement that we wouldn't ever go to sleep at night mad at each other. That's why the past few months had been so devastating for me; it was totally out of character for Scott to be acting the hateful and selfish way he had been acting.

Of course, it didn't take a rocket scientist to figure out that the change in Scott coincided with our adopting Patrick. One thing I did know for sure was that Scott hadn't been all that excited about adopting a baby. But, truthfully, since he had eventually agreed to the adoption, I thought he had come to terms with his reservations about us having kids. I found out later, I could not have been more wrong. He emphatically did not want children because he didn't want to share his home or me with anything, including kids.

The instant the social worker placed little Patrick in my arms, something evidently snapped in Scott. I guess the reality of the adoption suddenly hit him. Without being able to say so, he was furious at me for wanting a baby — that was the long and the short of it.

Scott had changed instantly. He was no longer the fun–loving, easygoing guy I had married and had, instead, turned into someone I didn't recognize. It was the same outer body, but everything inside him had changed, and not for the better either.

I despised him for the way he had brushed us aside all those months. He had acted as though neither of us existed. I was sixteen–hundred miles away from my family. Alone really, except for Scott's family, and while they knew something of how he was acting, they had no idea how bad things really were between us.

Chapter 4

In the beginning I felt powerless, but not now. Not after months of Scott treating us the way he had. Although I was terrified of being exposed, I was now empowered by the knowledge that only a year separated me from this miserable existence with Scott and complete happiness with Kathleen. I knew that if I could tough it out for one more year, I would be free of Scott, his family, the church, and the whole self-righteous community.

However, in order to keep everything from falling apart, I had to learn to conquer my fear so I could act naturally. Then, out of nowhere there had been a new and what I thought was a dangerous development. After all the months of completely rejecting us, Scott had made a total about-face and wanted his family back. He apologized over and over for the way he had behaved. He said he wanted to pick up the pieces and go on; he wanted all of us to act as if nothing had ever happened.

Scott said that he wanted to be a father to Patrick and he wanted to resume his rightful place as husband in my life. He actually wanted to be intimate with me again. I can tell you for certain that it was much, much too late for that. Even the thought of sleeping with him made me sick to my stomach.

The truth was that I wanted nothing to do with Scott anymore, but Patrick's adoption wouldn't be final for twelve months. Pretending to be a wife to him, even on the surface, was almost more than I could endure, but I could not risk losing my precious little Patrick.

Maybe I could convince Scott that I needed time to think so he would quit pestering me. *Yes, that was it,* I thought. *I will try to talk to him along those lines, but in no way could he ever know what was really happening between Kathleen and me.*

Just then Scott came home and I blurted out, "Scott, we need to talk." He was more than happy that I wanted to talk. I guess he thought it was a promising first step. I explained to him that so much had happened that I needed time to think. I told him that I needed time to work through my feelings. And I told him I needed some space, and anything else I could think of to make him quit hounding me.

How I made what I said believable, I'll never know, but, somehow, he actually believed me. I guess he thought that since he had been acting so mean and hateful that maybe he could give me a week or two to pull myself together. I really don't know what he was thinking, and I didn't really care as long as he backed off and gave me the space I needed to figure out what to do with this new revolting development.

Since he had been badgering me about resuming our life for a couple of weeks with no positive movement from me, he said, "Okay, but do you have any idea about how long it will take?" How insane was that?! He had basically ignored his wife and son for months, but now that *he* decided it was time to get back together, I was supposed to forgive him and welcome him back with open arms. Although his whole attitude about the situation really irritated me, I was glad that at least some of the pressure would be lifted, if only for a little while.

Truthfully, just to get some of the immediate crushing weight off my shoulders was a tremendous relief. Kathleen and I could use this reprieve, however long it was to be, to try and come up with a plan that would enable me to endure the miserable situation until we could legally move away with Patrick.

One thing was for damn sure, though, I was not going to have sex with Scott. Whatever plan we came up with had to figure that in as one of the top considerations. So far, I had been able to put off his advances by saying I wasn't ready, too much had happened, I needed time, and similar things. But from the way Scott was pushing for a full reconciliation, Kathleen and I both knew that time was running out for me, and really for both of us. Kathleen could not bear the thought of my sleeping with him either.

Kathleen and I loved each other passionately. Even under these strained circumstances our love remained strong, vibrant, and beautiful. Just to be near each other made us both happy and we couldn't wait to be together permanently away from this sanctimonious town and all its small-mindedness.

Chapter 5

Kathleen had a small apartment close to campus, and Patrick and I were going up there tomorrow afternoon for the weekend. I can't tell you how much I was looking forward to being alone with her again. Even thinking about her beautiful, sweet face made me smile. Kathleen made me feel things that I had never dreamed possible. Our eyes sought each other whenever we went into any room and even the slightest casual brush of her hand on mine could set us both on fire.

Actually, that was one of the reasons why I'd been so upset and fearful lately. It was becoming increasingly more difficult for Kathleen and I to act like we were only casual friends when we were at church for the Sunday morning service and our Sunday school class. I was terrified that one of us would slip and give our secret away.

For me, just being in the room with her when other people were around was extremely risky. I could no longer look at her innocently like I had before we became lovers. I felt that it was a real possibility that some telling look from either of us would expose us to the world. Neither one of us was good at acting, but I was the one who wasn't particularly good on my feet.

Maybe people couldn't tell, but I just knew that everyone could see that there was something going on between us. If just one of the old holier-than-thou gossiper's got wind of anything suspicious, it would not only be the scandal of the county, it would destroy my chances for keeping Patrick, to say nothing of what it would do to our families. No, we had to put on the show for a little while longer and that was all there was to it.

But, thankfully, we were going to have this weekend together. Even though Scott had made a 180-degree turn as far as being a husband and a father, he had a golf tournament commitment somewhere, so I didn't have to worry about him. I would be free for the weekend. Kathleen and I were both ecstatic that we were going to have a couple of days together. While we were both worried about the looming situation, she had faith that, together, we could come up with a plan that would pull us through.

Kathleen was waiting for us when Patrick and I got to her apartment. She was standing outside her front door on the landing at the top of the stairs. When she saw my car turn into her parking lot, she flew down the stairs and was at my window almost instantly. She was there before I even thought about getting the door open.

I rolled down the window; Kathleen's soft green eyes betrayed her worry. My eyes met her questioning gaze honestly. *No, my love, nothing has changed; we are safe. Our love is still intact. I love you with every cell of my being, and I always will. Stop worrying. It's okay.* My eyes were doing their best to reassure her. I didn't want her tormented, not for a second longer.

It seems impossible that just one momentary look could put to rest so much uneasiness, but in that quick silent exchange, all of her disturbing questions were answered. Satisfied, her fingertips brushed my bare forearm. Her shoulders visibly relaxed. Glad to see the concern fade from her beautiful, precious face, I wanted to pull her to me and hold her right there on the spot, but something like that simply could not happen in public.

We were two homosexual women living in a straight world. We had to think about what we were doing and who we were every second we were outside of Kathleen's small apartment. Inside her apartment was the only place we really felt we could be safe and free. Such was the political climate of the mid sixties.

Kathleen had everything planned and ready for us to have a perfect romantic weekend together. It had been a few weeks since we had been alone together. Since she knew what a terrible time I'd been having lately, she wanted to make it extra special for all of us.

Because Scott had been an absent father, Patrick had grown very fond of Kathleen. She had four younger siblings and had an easy, special way with little ones. Actually, due to her experience, I'll have to admit she was really better with Patrick than I was.

She had bought some rib-eye steaks and we were going to grill them outside after we fed Patrick and got him settled in for the night. Her apartment was on the second floor of an older brown, brick building that was filled mostly with grad students and retired people. We typically grilled out on her tiny balcony, which overlooked a small, grassy, shaded park where we took Patrick to play when we were in town.

That evening, after we lit the charcoal in the grill, we put on some music and pushed the coffee table to the side so we could dance. We both liked to dance, but we particularly loved to slow dance. Kathleen was a good dancer and usually took the lead.

That night, dancing was secondary; we just wanted to be as close as we could possibly be. Neither of us even pretended to lead on this very special Friday evening.

As soon as the music started, our bodies melted into each other and our lips met, instantly igniting a sweet, urgent passion. We swayed easily with the slow beat of the music. We'd probably heard the lyrics a thousand times before, but they still stirred the same sensual feelings that they always had. We wanted each other now, right now; waiting was no longer an option.

Kathleen wore her gorgeous sandy-blond hair up in a ponytail that afternoon. She'd been playing tennis earlier that day. I liked her hair up, but I absolutely *loved* it down. I thought it was sexy the way it fell in my face when she was perfectly naked and lying on top of me. Her hair was one of the things that turned me on about her and she knew it.

Without a word from me, Kathleen deftly undid her ponytail, shook it out, and then just stood there grinning one of those marvelous, mischievous grins of hers. That was my cue; she certainly didn't have to undo anything else.

I began to unbutton the light blue, checked shirt she was wearing. I slowly unbuckled her belt and unzipped her slacks. As we kissed, I pushed her shirt back off one shoulder and then the other. I slipped my fingers under her bra strap and worked my hand down to the clasp in the back. The bra silently dropped to the floor. Kathleen had a beautiful body, flawless really. I loved every inch of her supple athletic frame.

She was stunning as she stood there before me like that. I could tell that she was deliberately tantalizing me. Her body promised what only she could deliver. At this particular moment, she totally controlled the situation, and me, with it. Intoxicated by her obvious teasing, her sensuous mouth, her sexy eyes, her long, beautiful, flowing hair, and her round firm breasts, I stood there drinking her in.

Finally, thinking that I'd had enough, Kathleen took pity on me. She reached out to put her hands around my neck to draw me to

48

her, but I was transfixed — I thought, *just give me a little more time to take in what I'm seeing, feeling, being.* Kathleen, knowing that it was somehow important, patiently held the scene for me. I will never, as long as I live, forget how she looked that day.

Finally, I regained my ability to move, and, unhurriedly, I pulled her to me. She was in my arms. Our lips met softly, tenderly, and then with utter crushing abandon.

She had nothing on now except her unzipped black slacks and a pair of really cute, little blue silk bikini panties. In one motion, we slipped to the floor. I helped her wiggle out of her slacks and bikinis. We both hurriedly took my clothes off, and then, finally, we were making delicious, passionate love there on Kathleen's living room floor.

By now we were more experienced lovers. We could hold her climax in abeyance while her body fully experienced her ecstasy. Kathleen was a thrilling, knowing lover; she repeatedly gave me fever-pitched multiple orgasms. We made love for hours that night and finally fell spent, completely satiated, in each other's arms.

We'd forgotten all about the charcoal and grilling the steaks. Neither of us minded, though. The hours we spent together that night were much more important than any steak or, for that matter, anything else in the world.

Chapter 6

The next morning after we fed Patrick, we put him in his swing and sat down at her small kitchen table to have a cup of coffee and try to figure out what to do about Scott and his new annoying advancements toward me.

We were both still scared to death that our secret would get out. Kathleen thought her mother would eventually deal with it, but she thought the news that his oldest daughter was a lesbian would kill her dad.

John Crutchfield was, himself, a product of the church and firmly believed that homosexuality was what the Bible called, "An abomination unto the Lord." He raised his kids to be God-fearing people. It would have brought shame and dishonor on him personally if something as ungodly as lesbianism showed up in his blood family — his kin.

My mother felt very much the same way. While I didn't give a shit about what my stepfather thought, I didn't want to bring ridicule and disgrace on my mother if I could help it. *Let sleeping dogs lie* was my thought about both our families. *What they didn't know wouldn't hurt them* was Kathleen's thought. We both felt it would better all the way around if we could just wait it out and keep on doing what we were doing until we could pack up and leave Paducah for good.

We were both feeling somewhat hopeless about our predicament, so I decided to lighten things up a little and tell Kathleen about how all my gossipy relatives back in Eudora felt about gay people in general and about homosexuals in the family in particular.

I told her about how the gossipers back home had talked about old Miss Flowers, the gym teacher, and old Miss Euler, the principal of the junior high school. It was a hot rumor that they were involved in something extremely unholy. The whole town talked about what a shameful terrible thing it was that it was going on right under the whole town's noses.

But when my nutty Aunt Grace on my mother's side of the family died, something happened at the wake that caused the community to gasp and tore our family completely to pieces.

50

One of her sons, Bruce, turned out to be gay. But thank the good Lord, Aunt Grace died in an awful car accident before Bruce dropped that dreadful bomb on the family; he let the cat out of the bag at his mother's funeral. He introduced his "life partner" at the funeral, or, actually, it was really at the wake. I guess poor Bruce was so distraught over his mother's death that he just couldn't help himself. Apparently, he just had to come clean.

He and his life partner, Tony, had been up to San Francisco for a few vacations, so they knew all the latest terms for the homosexual life style it seemed.

The news wasn't really a big surprise to my mother, my grandmother, all of my aunts, and the older girl cousins because, unbeknownst to Aunt Grace, when she would dare miss one of the family hen parties, the rest of them had all been whispering behind her back about the possibility of Bruce being "that-a-way."

As a child, I'd hear one of them say, "Look at the way he sort of swishes when he walks, the way he flips his hands sometimes, and that girly way he talks is so embarrassing. Lord, help us all; I hope it's not really what we think it is."

And then, my Aunt Georgia would chime in, "Bless her heart! Grace has got enough on her plate as it is without him turning out like that." Though all my female family members had been expecting that the terrible truth would eventually come to light, they were totally mortified and outraged that Bruce spilled the beans right in front of the whole community at his own mother's funeral. As you can imagine, from then on in, there was enough kitchen-table babble to last for eternity.

My uncles and all the older male cousins were, at first, confused about Bruce's untimely announcement, but when it finally did begin to sink in, my Uncle Bob said, "Hell! Is he saying they are queers?"

Aunt Georgia, Uncle Bob's wife and the worst gossiper in the whole county or maybe even the whole state, said, "Yes, Bob, I'm pretty sure your dead sister's son and your blood nephew said that he is a homosexual."

Uncle Bob's face turned beet red. He fairly glared at her. Then he turned on Aunt Georgia, who was at least a foot shorter than he was, and shouted at the top of his lungs, "Don't you ever let me hear you say anything like that again, do you hear me?"

Aside from being short, Aunt Georgia had one of those strange looking duck butts. You know, the ones that are flat and kind of turn up in the back. To top that off, she had some kind of a hip problem that caused her to walk waddle-style, exactly like a duck.

Personally, I don't think Aunt Georgia had ever seen my Uncle Bob get that fired up over anything. As recall, I think she was awfully afraid for a minute or two that he was going to punch her out or something; as if he hadn't already embarrassed and humiliated her enough to last from now to eternity as it was.

To save as much face as she possibly could, Aunt Georgia, gathered her wits about her, mustered her courage, straightened her shoulders, stuck her nose up in the air, gave her ample upturned behind a couple of wiggles, turned on her little short black heels, and slowly waddled out of the room.

Well! Everyone at the wake, which was pretty much the whole darn family and most of the church members, had heard my Uncle Bob shout at Aunt Georgia. He sounded for all the world like a wounded, raging bull. The way he was snorting and blowing and roaring, and the way his face was all red and screwed up, there was just no way anyone could have missed the frightful scene.

The room fell deathly silent — no pun intended —you could have heard a pin drop from a thousand paces. All of us kids were afraid to speak, and we didn't move a muscle. We were waiting for a cue from the adults as to what to do next.

The adults were mostly stoned-faced, but some of them were trying their best not to snicker. They looked back and forth at each other for the briefest of moments, then they dropped their heads. One by one, every last man woman and child, all of them except for Aunt Grace's six other children who were gathered around their mother's casket, shuffled out the front door in single-file as orderly as could be.

Bruce was the next-to-youngest son. His oldest brother, JP, was a CIA or FBI agent or had some kind of secret important job with the government; none of us knew exactly what he did. All of Bruce's siblings were shocked and shamed by the news that their brother was a homosexual, but JP was absolutely livid. When his brother confessed his real sexual identity, JP looked as if someone had taken a saber to his very own masculinity.

I felt real sorry for all of Aunt Grace's kids. In spite of Aunt Grace's crazy ways, her kids loved her, and they were really grieving up there as they stood around her open casket. Poor kids! Now besides losing their kooky mother, those kids had to be saddled with this kind of embarrassment for the rest of their born days.

I peeked in Aunt Grace's coffin as we were all filing out the front door just to see if she was still face up, but, no, nothing had changed. She was still lying there, nose pointed toward the ceiling. Her head was propped up on one of those little pink pillows they used in the caskets back then.

In my young mind, it proved that people don't actually turn over in their graves, or Aunt Grace would have flipped over for sure at that bit of appalling news Bruce decided he just had to share at her funeral.

At the time, that was the worst stink our family had ever dealt with. But, thankfully, there was one tiny bit of saving grace for the rest of the relatives; it was one of Aunt Grace's sons and not one of their own strapping boys that had brought that kind of shameful humiliation on the family.

Bruce was on my mother's side of the family, but there was similar shameful trouble on my father's side. My Uncle Mike, my dad's youngest brother, was the best-looking guy around but he didn't go for the girls. So, of course, the relatives on both sides thought and whispered that he was surely homosexual. Uncle Mike was a pilot in the war and was a decorated hero. But all the same, he was only mentioned at family events as a filthy, lowdown queer.

At the time, I remember thinking several times that I was mighty glad that my sisters and I were budding saints ourselves, and none of us would ever have to worry about giving that gaggle of babbling gossips any kind of a scandal to prattle about.

My reminiscing about my childhood memories of family homosexuality had made my beautiful Kathleen smile, in fact, she was flat out laughing thinking about the sight of Bruce up there in front of his mother's coffin introducing his "life partner" and laying his sexual identity out for the whole world to see.

Chapter 7

While we were drinking our coffee and laughing, Bobbie, a college friend of Kathleen's, came bopping in. She was one of the very few people who knew about Kathleen, and she was the only one who knew that Kathleen and I were seeing each other. I was terrified that she knew about us, but Kathleen assured me that Bobbie was not only her best friend, but also lesbian, and could be trusted to keep our secret.

Bobbie's dad owned the only Insurance agency in Paducah where almost everyone in town got their business, home, and auto insurance. Because Scott and I had our insurance there, I already knew Bobbie, but it wasn't until Kathleen let her in on the fact that we were seeing each other that I found out that Bobbie was a lesbian, too.

Since she already knew, we filled her in on the latest troubling development. We thought maybe she would be able to offer some advice on how to deal with Scott's new lovely-dovey attitude toward the baby and me. "God," she said as she sipped her coffee. "You two really have a mess on your hands, don't you?"

We agreed that we did, and the three of us tried to think of something, really anything, that would stall Scott for the next twelve months. What we needed was for Scott to stay in the marriage until the final adoption papers were signed. We all decided that the only thing that was going to help us was a real, live, modern-day miracle.

Later that evening, Scott called me at Kathleen's apartment. He was all excited and wanted me to come back home immediately. He wouldn't tell me over the phone what was up, but he assured me that he had terrific news that he wanted to tell me in person.

Kathleen and I were understandably upset that our weekend had been cut short. But in order not to raise suspicion, we agreed that I should drive back to Paducah. We were both heartbroken; we treasured every moment alone together and to have it interrupted like this … well, I think we were both afraid that it was an example of the kind of thing we could expect for the next twelve months.

When Patrick and I got home, Scott was anxiously waiting for us. In fact, when he saw our car pull in the driveway, he came out to help with my bag, Patrick, and all of his stuff. Bouncing around the room like someone who had just won the million-dollar question, he could hardly wait to tell me his good news.

It seemed that he had played golf with Mr. Winters that day. Mr. Winters was an older businessman who owned one of those independent local motels and restaurants; you know, the type that you see in almost every small town, not ratty looking, but not fancy like the big chains either. Mr. Winters was also a deacon in our church and he knew that Scott had wanted to get out of the Air Force and settle down in Paducah.

While they were out on the golf course, Mr. Winters made Scott a surprising offer that Scott didn't think we should refuse. I didn't know what *we* meant, but, anyway, I was listening. It seemed that Mr. Winters needed to retire for health reasons and wanted Scott and I to take over his motel and restaurant business right away.

Right off the bat, there were three huge problems to his proposition. One, we had a baby, which severely limited my time. Two, Scott was the Air Force recruiter for the area and still had a year or so left on his military contract. Three, neither of us knew anything whatsoever about the motel and restaurant business. I would be the one that would shoulder the majority of the load until Scott's service term was up.

Scott was on top of the world over the offer. We would be making more money as a base salary than Scott was making in the Air Force, and we would also make a percentage of the profit. I had to admit that it was a pretty sweet deal financially, except for all the major problems I just mentioned.

I could tell by the sheepish way Scott was acting that he expected me to say no, but the wheels in my mind were spinning ninety miles an hour. I came to the conclusion very quickly that this was the answer to my prayers. This was the miracle we had been hoping for; I thought, *this timely proposition might actually work!*

We would have to move into the living quarters over the motel, which would allow me to manage it in the daytime and also take care of little Patrick. Scott would have to work the front desk at night, which would leave zero time or opportunity for us to have a romantic reconciliation.

I didn't care how hard I had to work if it would give me the time I needed for Patrick's adoption to go through. I told Scott that, although it would be really difficult for us until he left the service, I thought we could manage with a lot of hard work on both our parts.

He was thrilled and grateful that I was willing to take it on, especially since he had been acting so mean and hateful. I did notice, though, that he didn't seem to be the least bit concerned about the amount of work it would take on my part, or how it would affect my ability to take care of Patrick. Nevertheless, I was all in.

I couldn't wait to tell Kathleen the terrific news, but I would have to wait until Scott left for work the next morning to use the phone.

Chapter 8

As soon as Scott's car hit the pavement the next morning, I was on the phone to Kathleen to tell her about the wonderful, awesome turn of events. She was immediately concerned that I would not be able to hold up and do it all but agreed that it was something that could buy us the twelve months we needed for Patrick's adoption to finalize.

We thought we wouldn't have as much private time together, but Kathleen could still come by the motel on Friday afternoons on her way home from school. Typically, Kathleen spent Sunday afternoons after church at my house, too. We didn't know how that would work out yet; we would have to wait and see.

Actually, things went pretty well. Scott, Patrick, and I moved into the living quarters over the motel. We hired a manager for the restaurant and I ran the forty-unit motel and took care of little Patrick. Kathleen came by to see Patrick and me on Friday afternoons like normal, but Sundays were guarded. Kathleen would come over to see me, but Scott was in and out all the time now. We never knew when he was going to pop in, so we made it a hard and fast rule to never be in any kind of a compromising situation.

We did have a lot of fun when Kathleen was at the motel visiting, even though we couldn't be intimate. The motel had one of those old phone systems where the guests had to go through the switchboard to make or receive a call. Whoever was in the office was pretty much tied to the old relic of a thing. Kathleen learned to operate it so she could help me when she was there.

Wives would call their husbands. When the husbands didn't pick up the phone in their rooms, the switchboard operator would get a nasty earful about how worthless the husband was. After a few futile attempts, sometimes a wife would say, "I know he is in there, can you go down to his room and knock on his door?" We did that many a time.

Typically, the husband would shamefacedly come to the door only to be told what he already knew. His wife had been calling and wanted to talk to him…and right now, too! Kathleen and I got a lot of good laughs during our tenure as motel switchboard operators.

The office/lobby area was a huge tiled space with lots of room for Patrick to play with his toys. Many of the customers were traveling salesmen, who considered our motel a home away from home and would come down to the lobby just to have fun with little Patrick. Word got around about what a clean, comfortable, friendly place we had, so the business really grew.

Under the circumstances, the twelve months passed fairly rapidly. Kathleen and I had made up our minds that I would tell Scott I wanted a divorce as soon as the final adoption went through. I was going to tell him that I just didn't love him anymore, and that I wanted to move on with my life. I was not going to tell him anything else. No, I would just say that I wanted out of our loveless marriage. Foolishly, I thought that would work.

Kathleen, just through with college, was helping her dad with his businesses, but when we moved, she was sure she could get a job in almost any big city. I knew how to type and take dictation, so I was confident that I could find work, too. In our minds, this horrible mess was very close to being over.

As the time got closer for Scott and me to meet before the judge to get Patrick's final adoption papers, Kathleen and I became more and more elated. At last, we would finally be together; the long wait was about over; our patience had paid off. We were about to truly be free to live our lives without the scrutiny and condemnation of our families and the prejudiced, self-righteous community we lived in. We were almost giddy with anticipation.

Chapter 9

True to our plan, the day after we got Patrick's final adoption papers in the mail, I told Scott that I wanted a divorce. Since he had two more months in the service, I told him I would stay to run the motel until he got his discharge, but he could move out into one of the motel rooms as of that very day.

I didn't see that it was going to be much of a big deal to Scott anyway. He still had very little to do with Patrick, and he knew that didn't set well with me. While we were cordial, we just passed in the stairway leading up to the living quarters. When he was on duty at the front desk, Patrick and I were upstairs, and when I was on duty, he was doing his Air Force recruiting job. That part had worked out just as I'd hoped it would.

I wasn't prepared for Scott's reaction. My God! You would have thought I had cut off his right arm or something. At first, he begged and pleaded and said he didn't want to lose his family. Then he said it would hurt his mom and dad and my family back in Eudora. He also talked about how it would look to the people in the church and the community. Finally, he even resorted to talking about how much our customers would miss Patrick and me being in the office when they checked in. Interestingly, he never once said that he loved Patrick or me.

After several hours of this and me standing firm, he began to get angry and really nasty and started to say awful things — blaming me for forcing Patrick on him and for destroying our home. Scott had once again turned into someone I didn't know, except this time he was enraged, maddened by the idea that I wanted to leave him even though our marriage had been over from the time we brought Patrick home from the adoption center. He acted like I was his property, and that I couldn't leave unless he said so.

He wanted to know if there was someone else. He kept quizzing me over and over until I finally yelled at him, "Yes, there is someone else!" He fell silent. I could tell that he was trying to figure out when I ever had the time to see or to talk to anyone else.

Completely clueless, he started accusing me of sleeping with the various salesmen that were regular guests at our motel. He went over the names of the men that came in once a week. Was it Jeff

Conrad? Or maybe it was Bill Hastings? Or maybe I had slept with all of them! His insults were increasingly vulgar and belittling to me.

At last, I was tired of being his whipping post and I said, "It is none of them, Scott. It's a woman who I'm in love with."

The color drained from his face when I said that; he looked like someone had hit him in the stomach with a baseball bat. I don't know what came over me, but then I calmly told him the truth that I'd been hiding for all these many months. He knew I wasn't just trying to get back at him because he knew how close Kathleen and I were, but all along he thought that Kathleen and I were only friends.

Scott flew out the motel lobby front door. I had no idea where he was going and, frankly, I didn't really care. At that moment, I was just glad to have it out and in the open so he would leave me alone and give me the divorce. Now, Patrick, Kathleen, and I could get out of there and have some sort of normal life.

Foolishly, I thought the worst was over. I went to bed thinking that things would be difficult for the next couple of months, but after that I would be free of the whole terrible, insane mess.

Nothing could have prepared me for what happened next.

Chapter 10

At first I thought it was a horrible nightmare, like the one I'd had as a child when I had dreamt my younger sister was burning up in a bedroom of our house.

That's the way it was that night. I woke up to someone choking me in my bed, but almost instantly, my mind went back to the horrifying dream of my childhood. For just a moment, I thought, *I'll wake up soon and this will be just a terrible dream.* But then my eyes opened and I clearly realized it was Scott, my husband, who actually had both hands around my throat. He was trying to choke me to death.

Pinned down by his heavy, sweating body, terror gripped me. He was applying crushing pressure to my neck, pounding my head up and down against the mattress and loudly cursing me all at the same time. I don't remember being in pain; I guess I somehow separated myself from the idea that I was actually being strangled to death.

It could not have been more than a few moments, but finally, instinctively, instead of continuing to submit to it like a rag doll, my basic will to live kicked in and I began to fight Scott back. When he raised himself up off my chest in order to put even more deadly pressure on my throat, I got one foot under his groin and kicked and shoved him with all my might. Furious and grabbing himself, he turned loose of my throat but dragged me off the bed by one arm and my long dark hair.

He dragged me toward the stairwell. As he kicked me down the stairs, he shouted despicable names at me. Thankfully, I can remember only a few of them, but they are forever etched in my mind. He called me a slut, a bitch, and a filthy fucking perverted lesbo. I was almost as shocked by the obscenities coming out of his mouth as I was by his actual physical attack. I'd never heard him talk like that before. In fact, being the son of a Southern Baptist minister, I didn't know that he even knew words like that.

I did not just tumble all the way down the stairs, but would catch myself every couple of steps only to be kicked again and again. Finally, my body reached the bottom. I have no idea what happened next, because I had thankfully blacked out just as I reached the floor of the motel lobby down below.

When I came to, Brother Allen and Polly, Scott's dad and mom, were standing over me and Scott was sitting on a chair near the front of the motel lobby door. Scott was distraught; he realized he had really hurt me, but because of his job in the Air Force, his position as the Choir Director in the church, his dad's position as minister, and his reputation in the community, he was afraid to call an ambulance and had, instead, called his parents.

In the way of small towns and close-nit Southern Baptist communities, the three of them had a vested interest in protecting their reputations separately and also as a group. I can honestly say that none of them except maybe, to some extent, Brother Allen cared one little bit about what had happened to me that night. I could see a glimmer of pain in Brother Allen's eyes, and I do think he felt sorry for me, but not sorry enough to buck his wife and his son.

From what I could make out in my dazed condition, they were conferring together as a group to see if it was absolutely necessary to take me to the ER. If not, they would try to patch me up at home, which is exactly what they did. Fortunately, nothing was broken, though I was bruised from one end to the other, and since I had lost consciousness, I had probably also suffered a concussion.

A long cut over one cheekbone and a smaller cut over the other eye already made it difficult to see. Their major concerns were the cuts on my face that were still bleeding quite a bit. Polly was dabbing at them with one of Brother Allen's handkerchiefs. The rest of my cuts, scrapes and bruises were on my torso, legs, and arms. My right arm was hurting like the dickens, but since I could move it, I thought it probably wasn't broken.

Scott had, at first, tried to say that I had slipped and fallen down the stairs, but the huge bruises on my neck told the real truth to his bewildered parents. The first words I heard when I regained my senses enough to really understand anything at all were from Scott's mother, Polly. She was saying that it would ruin them if word got out that their son had beaten up his wife, and Scott was saying, "Mama she deserved it, you don't know what she's done to me." Polly was scared to death to hear what I'd done to deserve what she was seeing. She didn't know her precious baby boy was capable of doing anything like this.

She had everyone in the church feeling sorry for her because of all her fake illnesses. Polly didn't want to lose all the attention she had been getting from the congregation members for those many years. I could tell her little mind was running as fast as it could to try come up with something, anything, to head off the repercussions of what had happened.

For a fact, she sure didn't want the church members and the rest of the community to know what Scott had done, and she sure didn't want them to know whatever it was that I had done to deserve it. Preachers were supposed to have exemplary families, and what she was seeing was far from that. This was no better than trailer park trash as far as she could see.

Scott blubbered, "She and Kathleen Crutchfield have been having an affair right under our noses. They are queers, Dad, that's what they are." Poor old Brother Allen and Polly were speechless. They had never in a million years expected anything like this. They both sat down to try and comprehend what Scott had just said. What did this mean? What would the fallout be?

John Crutchfield, Kathleen's father, was the head deacon in the church, the church where all of us went. It sounded like something that was shaping up to be the worst scandal our little community of Bible-thumping believers had ever seen.

Chapter 11

Scott's dad told him that he could never let anything like this happen again. He said, "Son, if you can't forgive her and live with her then leave her, but I don't want to ever see anything else like this again."

Scott said, "She doesn't want to be forgiven, she wants a divorce so she and Patrick can move away with that bitch. But I've fixed that, I've just been over to Deacon Crutchfield's house and told him to keep his daughter away from my wife." Polly and Brother Allen were slack-jawed at this last bit of terrible news. Now, public embarrassment was almost a surety.

Scott's mother was the first one able to convince her mouth to function, "What did John say?" Polly asked.

Scott replied, "He said to 'get away from his door and never come back.' Then he slammed the door in my face." From all their years together serving in the church, Brother Allen knew John Crutchfield pretty well. He knew that, at the very least, this meant that John would take his family and never darken the door of their church again. It might even mean a split in the church, but he also knew that under no circumstances would John want this shameful news to get out. So maybe there was still some way to contain the whole mess.

I guess I thought Scott would just let me go away quietly. After all, he didn't love either Patrick or me; he just didn't want to lose the perfect home he never had — a place to come and go, eat his meals, keep his clothes, and take showers was all I could see.

But it was much more than that. If I had been having an affair with a man, that would have been scandalous, but my taking a lesbian lover somehow emasculated Scott. He was furious at the thought of it. Most likely, he could hear his buddies at the golf club making fun of him.

I had no idea that Scott was going to run over to the Deacon's house as soon as I told him that I loved Kathleen. Horrified that he had done that, my main concern was how it was affecting Kathleen. Because of what Scott said to John Crutchfield, the one thing that Kathleen was afraid of had happened; her dad now knew and even in the condition I was in, I felt horribly responsible.

What was Kathleen thinking? What was she doing? What was happening over at her house? I needed desperately to talk to Kathleen to see what was going on, but there was no way I could call her with these three hovering around. Then I started to think that things might be as bad over at her house as they were here at my place, and she wouldn't be able to talk to me either. I didn't think John Crutchfield would hit his daughter, but then I didn't think what had just happened to me was a remote possibility either.

While the three of them talked, I laid there on the lobby floor. Finally, they realized that a customer could walk through the motel lobby door at any minute. Brother Allen helped me up the stairs and into my bathroom where I could survey the damage. After she knew that I'd been having an affair with Kathleen, Polly acted as if I was a leper. The sight of me disgusted both her and Scott. The feeling was mutual that was certain; I couldn't stand to look at either of them, either.

I told Brother Allen to keep Scott away from me. "Scott can move into one of the motel rooms until I get well enough to get Patrick and me out of here," I said. While I didn't have much leverage left, I had overheard and already knew enough to understand that all of them wanted to keep this whole ugly situation as contained as they possibly could.

Scott and his family now knew our secret. Since Scott had gone absolutely berserk, the Deacon Crutchfield knew. And now that it was out in the open, we could all come to terms with what to do next.

That night, I bolted the door to the upstairs living quarters and tried to clean myself up. I wasn't sure about the cuts on my face, but I butterflied them as I best I could with some of the smallest adhesive bandages that come in the variety tin. I took some aspirin and tried to sleep, but all I could think about was what an awful mess I'd made of everything. *If only I had kept my big mouth shut when Scott was badgering me, none of this would have happened.* Most of all, I felt terrible that Scott felt the need to tell Kathleen's dad. She had always said she thought it would destroy him.

Chapter 12

Since Scott was still in the Air Force and had to work the next day and I looked like I'd been run over by a train, Brother Allen came over to man the desk. He had manned the office for us a couple of times before, so he was familiar with how things went.

About 10 a.m., Brother Allen came up the stairs to talk to me. When I saw his ashen face, I knew something terrible must have happened. He said, "Mandy, John Crutchfield is dead of a massive heart attack."

"Oh my God!" I said. I needed to go to Kathleen but in my condition, I didn't dare go. As far as the church community knew, I was Kathleen's best friend. I would be expected to be there for her and my absence would be noticed, but maybe people would think that Patrick was sick or something.

I didn't know for sure if she knew that Scott had been to her parent's house the previous night to tell her father to keep her away from me. There was still a possibility that John had just opened the door, listened to what Scott said, and repeated it to no one. I needed to talk to her desperately to see exactly what had happened and how she was. What had Scott done? What had I done? What had we done? I'd never felt so guilty in my life.

Brother Allen was obligated to go to see the Crutchfield family immediately. That was the first thing the preacher did when one of his congregation passed. I couldn't go down stairs to work because of the shape I was in, so we decided to call Shirley, a lady who worked for us part-time. Fortunately, she could come on short notice. Brother Allen told her that he had to leave and that I was upstairs with the flu. Strange how preachers lie when they need to, isn't it?

Before Scott's dad left, I asked him to please let me know how the Crutchfield family and Kathleen were doing. He said that he would. I was beside myself with worry about everything that had happened, but I was especially worried about Kathleen. She was very close to her dad. From when my beloved grandmother died, I knew that Kathleen would be in suffocating shock right now. She and her whole family would be devastated. So much had gone wrong that it seemed like a terrifying nightmare that would never end.

Now that Kathleen's dad was gone, what would she do? Would she ever want to see me again if she knew that I was the one who told Scott our secret? How was I going to contact her if her family knew that Scott had been to see her dad the night he died? Would they all be blaming Scott and me for the Deacon's death? Would Kathleen's family hold her responsible? For that matter, how was I going to be able to contact Kathleen with Scott now knowing the whole truth? All these questions and many more kept circling round and round in my throbbing head.

I had to find a way to talk to Kathleen. I wanted to help her, to be there for her, but that was impossible right now. I was literally a prisoner in my own home because of the horrible shape I was in. What if John Crutchfield had argued with Kathleen and that was what had caused his heart attack? There were simply no answers to any of my questions. I just had to wait to hear from Brother Allen.

I knew with all my heart that Kathleen and I loved each other, but even so, could our relationship survive the devastating disaster that our love had seemingly caused? I didn't know; all I could do was wait for Brother Allen to get back from his pastoral visit over at the Crutchfield's. At this point, any news at all would help.

Mandy Episode 3

Chapter 1

Worried out of my mind, I paced back and forth in front of the double windows of our living quarters above the lobby of the Bluegrass Motor Lodge, the small 40-unit independent motel that my husband, Scott, and I managed. From my vantage point, I could easily see every vehicle that entered or exited the motel parking lot. One thing was certain, if I could help it, I would not be taken by surprise again ... ever.

Questions that I desperately needed answered circled around my head like a bunch of pesky houseflies. Until I found out exactly what had happened over there, I knew that I could not make a move in any direction. Right now my hands were tied, regardless of how much I didn't like it.

Waiting for Scott's dad, Brother Allen, to come back from the Crutchfield home took every bit of what little patience I could muster. But no matter how frustrating the wait, I simply had to restrain myself from doing anything until I heard the news I hoped my father-in-law would soon bring me.

Patience has never been one of my virtues, and it was certainly no different on this God-forsaken day. *Mandy, you just have to wait; there is absolutely nothing you can do until you hear firsthand what is going on,* I lectured myself.

I wanted to know how Kathleen and her family were doing after the death of John Crutchfield, Kathleen's father. I wanted so much to go to Kathleen myself, or at least call her, but that was out of the question under the present scandalous circumstances. For one thing, I looked like I had been beaten ... because I had. For another, aside from beating me, my husband had, in a vicious, jealous rage, done a horrible, unforgivable thing.

To make matters worse, I caused the entire disastrous chain of events myself. After Scott badgered and belittled me for hours, I finally blurted out to my husband of seven years that I was in love with a woman. Then, with steely composure, I brazenly told him who the woman was and even when we started the affair. That was when all hell broke loose.

I really couldn't see why it mattered to Scott since, for many months, he had been treating Patrick, our precious little adopted baby, and me as if we didn't exist. He had never set foot in little Patrick's room nor had he ever held him.

It became clear much later that he had been punishing me for bringing our beautiful angel into our home. Forcing little Patrick on him, as he saw it.

It was during this awful period of rejection when Kathleen waltzed her gorgeous self into my life. Truthfully, until I'd fallen in love with Kathleen, I'd never thought such happiness was possible. What did she bring to my life? Excitement, passion, fun and the sure realization that joy wasn't just a word, but, rather, it could be a constant state of being.

In fact, the only reason that I hadn't already asked Scott for a divorce and moved off with Kathleen was that Patrick's adoption wasn't yet final. I needed the marriage to be intact, at least on the surface, in order for the judge to grant the final adoption papers.

I guess I thought that since Scott didn't love or want us, what possible difference would it make to him where and with whom Patrick and I went. Because of our positions in the community and in the church, I foolishly thought that Scott and his family would be more than happy — they might even be anxious — to see us quietly move away; the scandal would be contained and we could all get on with our lives. That would be the end of it.

I simply couldn't imagine the minister's family wanting the public embarrassment of the entire community finding out that the head deacon's daughter and I, the wife of the choir director and also the daughter-in-law of the preacher, were involved in what our church and community believed was an unholy, God-forbidden relationship.

Our Southern Baptist church, and most typical Bible Belt communities, strictly forbade what Kathleen and I felt for each other. People were routinely fired for being gay, children were legally taken from lesbian mothers, gays were humiliated and literally drummed out of the military, and if it was discovered that a tenant was a homosexual, it was grounds for immediate eviction from any rental property.

Of course, in most smaller towns and communities there would be the odd rumor of the existence of one or two gays, but talk like that was just mainly fodder for back fence gossiping. Since homosexual was thought to be the worst thing you could possibly be, there were no people openly living a gay lifestyle.

Waiting for Patrick's final adoption papers to come through was the only thing that had kept me in my loveless marriage and living in this particular Bible-thumping, small-minded community. Unfortunately, in our state it took eighteen months for any adoption to be final.

After my divorce, Kathleen and I had planned to take Patrick and move away to a big city where no one would know us, and where we could live unnoticed, safe, and free. Neither of us looked like your stereotypical lesbian, so it would be easy for us to get any apartment as just two girlfriends living together and sharing expenses. As you might imagine, we couldn't wait to get away from Paducah. Our moving away from the hate-filled atmosphere was the main topic of conversation when Kathleen and I got to spend any time alone together, which wasn't very frequently.

True to the plan, the day after Patrick's final adoption papers arrived in the mail, I told Scott that I wanted out of our marriage since I no longer loved him. Basically — and we both knew it — our life together ever since we adopted Patrick had become miserable for both of us. So it came as a complete shock that Scott adamantly wanted us to stay married. It was mind boggling to me; I just didn't get it.

At first he begged and pleaded, and then he grew increasingly more agitated and accusatory. Finally, there were the long hours of vulgar haranguing, where he accused me of sleeping with literally all the salesmen who frequented our motel. When something snapped and I'd had enough, I told him the truth. It was as simple as that — no excuses — just the honest-to-God truth. I, his wife, was a lesbian, and, furthermore, I very much liked being one.

That was when Scott went absolutely berserk. He flew out the door of the motel lobby. His red pickup truck screeched out of the parking lot literally on two wheels as he made the sharp right turn onto the pavement. I was surprised that the old truck still had that much pep as it bucked and fishtailed down the highway. I didn't know where Scott was going, and, frankly, I didn't care. I was just glad to finally get the whole business off my chest so I could find some peace.

Had I known where Scott was going and what he was doing, I would have been frantic and I would have tried, at least, to get in touch with Kathleen to give her a head's up on the fact that I had just blabbed our forbidden secret to Scott; the secret we had been carefully guarding for months.

Livid, Scott drove over to Kathleen's house and told John Crutchfield, her father and also the head deacon of our church, to keep Kathleen away from me. After Scott told Mr. Crutchfield, he came back to our living quarters and tried to strangle me to death as I slept. When I fought him back, he kicked me down the stairs; that was why I now looked like I had gotten the short end of a big stick. And that was why I never intended to let my guard down with him again. Lord! It wasn't even safe to go to sleep with him on the loose.

Everything was just a tangled mess now that I had told my husband the truth. I'm a person who likes answers, and this situation had a lot of questions that demanded answers.

Since, according to Scott, he had not been invited into John Crutchfield's house that night, I didn't know if anyone besides John had heard what Scott said to him. From what Scott indicated, John had calmly listened to what Scott had to say and then demanded that he leave and never come back without ever inviting him in. From my dealings with Scott lately, though, I had no reason to believe that Scott's account of what had happened was the whole truth or just the convenient truth according to Scott Allen.

Had Scott's hateful warning to John Crutchfield been what caused the heart attack that killed him? Did Kathleen know that I was the one who had told Scott our secret? If so, would she ever want to see or talk to me again? Had Kathleen and her dad gotten into an argument after Scott left? How was Kathleen dealing with the death of her father? What did her dad's death mean as far as our relationship was concerned? But most of all, for God's sake, I wanted to know if our love was still intact.

That was why I was so anxiously waiting for Brother Allen to get back from the Crutchfield's. He had gone over there as soon as he got the word that John had passed. As the minister, it was required of him to go to the home of the deceased to offer comfort and prayer. I asked Brother Allen to let me know how things were over there as soon as he got back. It had been hours now; I couldn't believe he was still over there. But, whether he was or wasn't, I had no choice other than to wait.

Chapter 2

Finally, from my upstairs window I saw Brother Allen's green, four-door Oldsmobile pull up in front of the motel office. Downstairs, the old oak lobby door swung open and then I heard it slowly creak shut. I heard voices coming from the motel office. No doubt, it was Shirley, our part-time desk help, and my father-in-law talking. In a few minutes, there were footsteps coming up the stairs and then a quiet knock on my door. I was already standing by the door with my hand on the knob when Brother Allen knocked.

I opened the door quickly and let Scott's dad into our living quarters: a small living room, one huge bedroom, a tiny room that we used for little Patrick's bedroom, a small bath, and a small galley kitchen.

Brother Allen took his old, gray, felt hat off and slumped down into one our overstuffed chairs. Though he had seen me several hours earlier, and even helped patch me up and get me back into our living quarters after Scott's brutal beating, I guess by now the bruises and cuts on my face and neck looked even worse than they had before he left to go visit the Crutchfield's.

Visibly shaken by what he saw, he slowly shook his head but made no other reference to it. Poor thing. In the seven years I'd known him, I had never seen the old minister looking so completely beaten. His eyes were cast down toward the floor; all I could see were his eyelids and the top of his balding head. He just sat there unconsciously picking at the green, tweed fabric on the top of the arm of the chair.

Unable to stand it a second longer, I finally said, "Dad, tell me what is happening over at the Crutchfield's."

"As you might expect, Mary and the children are all grieving for their loss, except for Kathleen. I didn't see Kathleen. I did ask Mary where she was and how she was doing. Mary said, 'Kathleen is in her room. She hasn't said a word since her father had the heart attack last night standing right over there in his study.'"

From what Brother Allen could gather, John suffered his heart attack the previous night sometime shortly after Scott completed his hateful mission. The ambulance was called, but John was pronounced dead upon arrival at the county hospital.

While Mary was obviously distraught over the death of her husband, she didn't seem to be at all antagonistic toward Brother Allen, Scott, or me. She had welcomed Brother Allen's prayer and spiritual comfort just as you might have expected any Christian mourning wife would do. They talked about what a good man John was and how he would be missed within the church and the whole community.

As was the custom, Mary Crutchfield, John's wife, wanted Brother Allen to officiate at John's funeral, and she wanted Scott, of all people, to provide the music for the funeral service.

To Brother Allen, it didn't sound like Mary or the rest of the family had heard what Scott said to John Crutchfield a few minutes before he was struck down by his fatal heart attack. He surmised that if Mary had known, she wouldn't have wanted Scott or Brother Allen to be a major part of her husband's funeral. In fact, between the two of them, they would provide all the officiating and most of the other programming for his final service.

Good Lord! This was shaping up to be the weirdest situation I had ever heard of!

But I thought, *If it were true that no one else in the family heard what Scott had to say, then there was also a good possibility that neither Mary nor the rest of the family knew that Kathleen and I were involved in the "forbidden sin" that had probably killed their husband and father.*

Additionally, from what Brother Allen said, I could reasonably assume that Kathleen did not know that Scott had said anything to her father or even that Scott had been to their home the previous night. She might have been in her room. It could have been anyone who knocked on the door. They had a large farm. It could have been one of the hired hands, or it might have been one of the managers from their businesses showing up to talk about a problem at one of the stores.

Suddenly, realizing that I was probably unwisely putting all that had happened in the most hopeful and promising light, I stopped myself from that line of thinking before it led to more optimism than was reasonably called for. But, at the very least, Brother Allen's report did seem to answer a few of my questions and it did give me a measure of hope. However, I still didn't know how Kathleen was;

and, from what Brother Allen was saying, she didn't know that I had told Scott about our secret.

We lived in a small community and the news of anyone's death spread like wildfire. Now that the whole town knew that John Crutchfield had passed, Kathleen was probably wondering why I had not come to her, if only as a friend. She had no way of knowing that Scott had beaten me right after he got home from telling her father to, " … keep your lesbian daughter away from my wife."

After Brother Allen left my living room, I decided to call Kathleen. My nerves simply wouldn't let me wait any longer, and also, admittedly, I was a little encouraged by my father-in-law's report. If it were as Brother Allen said, then there would be no reason why I couldn't at least talk to Kathleen. At any rate, I would just have to take the chance; I simply had to talk to her and that was all there was to it.

A mature, female voice unknown to me answered the phone at the Crutchfield's. I courteously gave my name and asked to speak to Kathleen. The voice said that Kathleen was in her room and would talk to no one, not even her mother. I asked the person to take down my name and tell Kathleen that I had called. Disappointed, I didn't know what else I could do at that moment. But now, at least, Kathleen would know I had tried to contact her. That brought a small measure of comfort to me.

I didn't know what shape she was in, but under the current circumstances, I could not go over to her house to see for myself no matter how much I wanted to. The moment she saw me, she would have known that something terrible had happened. Again, my hands were tied; I would just have to wait — my very least favorite thing to do.

Chapter 3

The local paper had a long write-up about John Crutchfield's life; how he had started from nothing and built and acquired several businesses in the area; how he ran a large farm and helped build the largest Southern Baptist church in the county. It recorded all of his survivors, including his wife, Mary, Kathleen, and her four siblings. He was a member of the Masons but had no hobbies to mention. The paper also said that he was a hard-working, self-made millionaire. *What? I knew they were well off, but I had no idea they were that wealthy.*

John Crutchfield was buried in our church cemetery. According to all accounts, the wake and the funeral went off without a hitch. All of John Crutchfield's family, except Kathleen, attended both of them. And most of the people in the church and in the community attended the services, as well; that is, all except me. Brother Allen officiated at the funeral and Scott sang a solo of "Amazing Grace."

What a hypocrite! It was so crazy that all those traditional rituals could go on without taking into account the horrendous thing that had happened, which had, in all probability, caused the poor man's death.

After the funeral, Scott, realizing that he had most likely killed Kathleen's father with his vicious, ill-fated warning, started to try to explain away his out-of-control conduct the night that I foolishly told him about Kathleen and me. To minimize what he had done to John Crutchfield, he claimed that he was out of his mind with jealousy.

Ridiculous! How can you claim to be jealous of your wife whom you have patently ignored for months? I thought.

To negate what he had done to me, he claimed that he didn't remember choking, kicking, and beating me. He said that he must have "blacked out or something." Of course, his parents wanted to believe him, but I knew that he could not have been more awake or more alert than he was when he was attacking me the night after he returned home from telling Mr. Crutchfield about Kathleen and me.

Unlike his parents, I didn't believe either of his ludicrous excuses for even a second. As far as I was concerned, it didn't matter how much backpedaling Scott did, the truth was that he knew that I knew that he was lying through his teeth.

I told Scott, "The next time you think about laying a hand on me, you better kill me, because if you don't I will find a way to kill you." From the look that I gave him and the way that I said it, he knew that I meant every word I said.

I made up my mind that no man, or for that matter anyone else, would ever abuse me and get away with it again. I might be in love with a woman, but I was still a human being; I did not have to lie down and take physical or verbal abuse from anyone.

With Patrick sitting on my lap, I made some serious promises to myself. Regardless of what had to happen, I would not let my little son see his mother being physically abused. Though he was too young to know what had happened this time, in the future, I didn't want him to grow up seeing and receiving the kind of abuse that I had been subjected to as a child. I promised myself that never again would I allow such a thing to happen to me, and it was a promise that I fully intended to keep.

After the funeral, Scott, Brother Allen, and Polly were all scrambling trying to ensure that they maintained their place in the church and in the community. They hoped against all hope that no one other than John Crutchfield had heard what Scott said the night he knocked on the Crutchfield's door.

At one point, I overheard Scott say, "If Kathleen just keeps her mouth shut, then we might still make sure their dirty, little secret doesn't get out."

Polly, Scott's mom, kept questioning Scott as to whether he could hear or see anyone else behind John as he stood at his front door listening to Scott's hateful warning the night he died. Scott didn't think that anyone else was in the room with John, but he couldn't be absolutely certain.

From the way Mary Crutchfield had acted toward Brother Allen and Scott, they thought it was highly possible that there was a very good chance that the scandalous bombshell was still contained. Now that John was dead, the only people left to know the forbidden secret were the three of them, Kathleen, and me, or so they thought anyway.

To outward appearances, Scott's dad, of course, sided with Scott and Polly, but as far as was possible, and without drawing too much attention to his kindnesses, he tried to help me as best he could the night of the horrific incident and afterward. He had tried to help me get myself patched up after Scott had kicked me down the stairwell that awful night. He privately brought me as much information as he knew as to what was going on over at the Crutchfield house. He told Scott that no matter what he could never resort to attacking me again.

But as for the other two, after all that had happened, I hated Scott and I despised his phony mother even more.

Polly, in a brainless effort to reconcile Scott and me, told me all about the intimate details of her life with Brother Allen. She told me how she really didn't enjoy sex either, but had learned to make the best of their life by throwing herself into praying to the Lord above, her church duties, reading the Bible, and quilting.

She, however, failed to mention how she avoided a good portion of her life by being on the fake-sick-list most of the time. Polly, the biggest hypochondriac in four counties, had probably used her many illnesses to avoid having sex with her husband. To hear her tell it, many Christian women she knew just pretended to enjoy sex for their husband's sake.

Polly made my stomach turn, and it was all I could do to keep from throwing her out of my home. I suppose she thought that I had turned to a woman because I couldn't deal with Scott's lovemaking. She obviously had no clue about anything that I was going through. She was right about one thing, though, I didn't like sex with Scott. In fact, no matter what I had to do, sex with him was a thing of the past.

Scott and his parents were cooking up something about a Christian Counseling Center in California that specialized in curing people of homosexuality. After my face healed up, they wanted me to consider going out there to see if the center could cure me of my horrible, unnatural disease. They said, "No one would have to know since you could stay with your sister and her husband who are stationed at the Marine base out there." I didn't think I had a disease, but if it came down to it, I might go out there just to get away from the three of them for a while.

Chapter 4

The day after the funeral, Mary Crutchfield, Kathleen's mother, unexpectedly came to the motel to see me. Because my face still looked too bad to be seen in public, I remained upstairs in the living quarters caring for Patrick and worrying myself silly about everything that had happened; I was especially worried about Kathleen.

Shirley called upstairs to tell me that Mary wanted to see me. I had no idea what was going on, but I thought that maybe Kathleen needed me. I really didn't know what to think, but I had no choice. I told Shirley to let her come up.

When I let Mary in, she was at once taken aback to see the shape I was in but with absolutely no hesitation, she sat down on the sofa to talk to me. She started right in telling me that it was all her fault about Kathleen. It had been she that had passed on the homosexual gene. According to Mary, her father's brother had carried the bad seed. Mary's side of the family was hoping the curse had ended with the brother, but Mary's father and mother knew from the time Mary was a teenager that she was the one in the new generation who harbored the shameful gene.

Mary knew she was different from other girls from the time she was a teen. She had wanted nothing to do with boys but her mother and father had forced her to marry John Crutchfield. She never loved John, but had been a good partner to him and had given him five children. According to Mary, she had not succumbed to the wiles of the devil and in so doing, she and her parents had hoped the family curse ended with her.

Obviously, as Mary told it, that was not to be. Even though she had sacrificed her inner feelings to thwart the devil and to be a good wife, the damning plague had visited itself on one of her offspring, her first-born, Kathleen. It was her firm belief that although she had hated it at the time, she had, nevertheless, done the right thing, the right and Godly thing. Now, she demanded of Kathleen that she do the same thing.

As Mary related the story, after Scott left their house that night John called Kathleen and Mary into his study. He told them what Scott had said at the door and asked Kathleen if it was the truth. Kathleen denied it at first, but after her father continued to press her, she finally admitted that she and I were in love with each other.

Her father became enraged and struck Kathleen hard across her face. Kathleen was badly shaken and stood there in total disbelief. As he raised his hand to hit her a second time, suddenly, something happened to him. He seemed to be in writhing, crushing pain. John desperately grabbed at his chest, stumbled backward and fell in a helpless heap to the floor. Mary called the ambulance; Kathleen went to her room and hadn't spoken since.

Mary wanted me to give her my word that I would, "never see or make any form of contact with Kathleen again."

I replied, "Mary, I can't do that. I have to see and talk to Kathleen myself."

Mary insisted, "I will not let the two of you ruin John's reputation and my family's good name. I have sacrificed everything to be where I am. If this dirty secret gets out, our whole family will be the laughing stock of the entire county. It is Kathleen's duty to do as I did. She will not live a lesbian life and that is all there is to it. I forbid it!"

My wits were about me enough that I questioned, "Is your reputation worth your daughter's happiness? Why can't Kathleen and I just move away together? No one here would ever have to know that we are together. Paducah isn't the only place where we can live. We had planned to move to a big city with Patrick after my divorce anyway."

Despite her own confession, she persevered, "No, Mandy, that won't be happening. I have already picked out a husband for Kathleen. Her remorse over her father's death will ensure that she does as I have planned. Although she hasn't said so, in fact, she hasn't said a single word, I know that she doesn't want to hurt me and her brothers and sisters anymore than she already has."

My brain was running ninety-to-nothing. I was thinking in little disjointed snippets:

John's death has really affected Mary mentally.

Kathleen is twenty-seven years old and not a child to be told what to do.

Mary is totally off her rocker if she thinks Kathleen will marry a man for any reason.

For God sakes, this isn't the dark ages where people believed that God punished the sins of the parents on the children for the third and fourth generations.

As soon as Kathleen gets better, she will contact me and we can decide how to get out of this insane situation.

Her mother has gone completely bonkers and needs some professional help.

But, for the immediate moment, I just wanted to get this crazy person, even if she was Kathleen's mother, out of my living room and out the door. I'd never heard anything so bizarre in my entire life, and I ushered Mary out of my home thinking, *Kathleen will straighten this all out as soon as she comes to her senses.* I was positive of that.

Even though Kathleen's mother had been acting somewhat psychotic during her visit, I had a better idea of what had actually happened the night that Scott told Kathleen's father to keep her away from me, or at least, I thought I did. Unfortunately, now there was one other person that knew about Kathleen and me. Now, the people that knew our forbidden secret were Kathleen, Scott, Polly, Brother Allen, and now Mary, and, of course, me.

Mary sure didn't want her daughter's secret to get out. Kathleen was overcome with grief and wouldn't be talking to anyone for a while it seemed. Scott, now that the damage had been done, didn't want to be the butt of jokes for the whole county, but especially for his golfing and macho, hunting buddies. Scott's parents would keep mum, as their future ministry and parsonage were at stake. That left me as the one, loose cannon.

I wanted to take Patrick and leave that whole part of the country, but I just couldn't leave without Kathleen. I had to wait for her to get over blaming herself for her father's death long enough to start thinking clearly. I didn't know how long that would take, but I was prepared to wait as long as I could possibly stand it. Waiting there in Paducah until Kathleen regained her ability to function normally was my plan. Then, I could see Kathleen and talk to her. I didn't know how, but I would find a way to be alone with her without her mother and the rest of her family hovering around like a bunch of heartless vultures.

She still loved me. I hoped that. I would not abandon her when she was out of her mind with grief. For now, I would just have to stay sane for the both of us.

Chapter 5

In spite of all the trauma in our lives, Scott and I had done so well with the motel and restaurant that we had investors wanting to back us to build a new motel and restaurant on the other side of town. The land for the new business was located right on the expressway. It was a sure-fire, can't-miss proposal. None of these investors, of course, knew of our marital problems, or that I was a lesbian, or they might not have been so anxious to put their money into this new venture.

Thankfully, Scott continued to live in one of the motel rooms, as I had demanded after the night that he attacked me. We all ate our meals in the motel restaurant. Patrick and I lived in the living quarters upstairs over the motel office and lobby.

Scott was on his best behavior after Mr. Crutchfield's funeral. He repeatedly asked me to forgive him for acting the way that he had, and he seemed to think that things could eventually return back to the way they were. In fact, he seemed to be trying to be the friend he had been to me before we got Patrick.

For my part, I wasn't saying anything one way or the other. I needed to stay in Paducah until Kathleen came around, and the status quo was working for me just fine while I waited. Looking back, I'm sure that Scott was encouraged, because not only had Kathleen seemingly dropped off the face of the earth, but I was also continuing to live at the motel and work as usual. He obviously thought my relationship with Kathleen was over but there were no outright conversations about the situation.

The restaurant manager quit and we brought my mother, Faith Ann, in from Eudora to manage the restaurant. Work had run out in Arizona and her stinking pervert of a husband came with her to find a job in construction, as well as my two sisters who were still at home. Vickie just graduated high school and would attend the community college; Nita, the youngest and Ed's daughter, was still in high school.

Little Patrick was more than two years old now and growing like a weed. From the time my feet hit the floor in the morning until I went to bed at night, I was busy. I intentionally filled my life to the brim so I didn't have to worry so much about Kathleen. And, mostly, I waited.

While I was forbidden to see Kathleen, Bobbie, her best friend in college, was able to get in to see her. Bobbie had graduated college and taken over a lot of the responsibility in her father's insurance agency, which was located right in downtown Paducah. Bobbie was herself a closeted lesbian, and the only one who knew I was continuing to wait on Kathleen.

Bobbie knew that Kathleen and I deeply loved each other, and she was trying her best to give me regular updates about Kathleen's state of mind. Every couple of weeks or so, she would visit Kathleen in her room at the Crutchfield home. Kathleen would just sit there staring without saying a word. It was the same exasperating report every single time, but by now, I had become an expert at waiting.

Kathleen's sister, Cheryl, married Joe Murray, one of our church members just out of college. He was an accounting major and since Kathleen had been sick, he had taken over the bookkeeping for the various Crutchfield businesses. Cheryl and Joe were expecting their first baby.

Out of the blue one day a few months after John Crutchfield passed away, Joe stopped in at the motel. He was all decked out in a suit, which was highly unusual for the men in our community unless it was Sunday and you were headed to church. I was a bit puzzled as to why he stopped in, but, nevertheless, I was cordial, thinking that he might have some word of Kathleen.

Joe talked pleasantly for a few minutes about a little of everything, including Kathleen. He said there was no change in her at all; she still sat silent in her room. Then, awkwardly, he started making lewd remarks to me; it seemed like he was trying to turn me on. Finally, more than a little irritated, I asked him what he was up to, and he told me that he knew the whole score; he knew about everything.

He knew about Kathleen and me and about Scott's visit to the Crutchfield house the night John Crutchfield suffered the heart attack. He had been coming around the corner of the house that night and overheard Scott telling John to keep his daughter away from his wife. While he hadn't actually been in the room when the heart attack occurred, he could guess what had happened. It was almost like he was trying to blackmail me into having sex with him.

Poor Joe. I'd been dealing with traveling salesmen far too long to let this little twerp of a bean counter get the best of me. I said, "Joe, go on back to your pregnant wife before I call Mary and tell her what her son-in-law has been up to." I wasn't worried at all about his stupid advances, but I was worried that this was yet one more person who knew. More than that, there was no telling how many other people blabbermouth Joe had already told our secret to.

It was hard to keep a secret of any kind in our small town, but it was next to impossible to keep one as juicy as this one. The fact that Joe knew our secret made me very nervous, but in reality, they could whisper and gossip all they wanted to, the fact remained that no one had ever actually seen Kathleen and I together in any sort of a compromising sexual situation. There was no actual proof; it was all hearsay.

Nevertheless, the rumors were making it increasingly more difficult for me to continue to live in Paducah. I wanted desperately to get out of there and away from the creeps and the gossiping. I was the same person with the same morals that I always had. It really maddened me that people would assume that I had changed into someone so immoral that I would do any kind of low-life thing.

Joe Murray wasn't the last one in our town to get the hots for me simply because it was rumored that I was a lesbian. Travis Stuart, a deacon in our church did practically the same thing. His clumsy, vulgar advances were particularly revolting because he, his wife, Doris, Scott, and I had been on the church bowling team, had played cards together, and had been guests in each other's homes.

One rainy afternoon, I was working the motel front desk when crazy-acting Travis came into the motel lobby and started rubbing himself right in front of me. He said he had been thinking about what it would be like to have sex with someone like me. I should have told him, "That's too bad, Travis, because I have never even once thought about what it would be like to have sex with someone like you." But I didn't. Instead, I told the very turned-on deacon that we should call Doris and see what she thought of the idea. Immediately, the lecherous smirk left his face and he couldn't get out the motel lobby door fast enough.

I guess for a straight, family man, having sex with a lesbian is the ultimate erotic experience. It must be a very strong fantasy for them to risk their reputations, their wives, and their children to fulfill a lewd, sexual dream. Or in the case of those two jerks, maybe they didn't think they would ever have another ready chance like that in the little town of Paducah.

Chapter 6

I spent my days waiting for Kathleen to come around, taking care of Patrick, managing the motel, taking classes with Vickie at the community college, and handling things at the restaurant when my mother and Scott were both out of pocket. Most days, there was never a minute to spare. At night, Patrick and I finally got to go upstairs to our little hideaway. After giving him a bath and tucking him into bed, I would finally have time to think about Kathleen.

I worried a lot about how she was doing and what they were doing to bring her back from wherever she had gone. It had been eight months since John Crutchfield's death. Was Kathleen ever going to regain her senses and her memory?

Many nights I fantasized about our last night together, the last one before I'd told Scott that I wanted a divorce. That last night alone together was extremely special to me, and I remembered it vividly.

We never allowed ourselves to be in an inappropriate situation when Kathleen came to the motel to see me, but, occasionally, Scott would go out of town to play in a golf tournament and Kathleen would come over to spend the night with Patrick and me in our living quarters. There was a huge dead bolt on the door, so I wasn't worried, and besides that, Shirley would be downstairs running the front desk.

On that very last night we were together, we were sitting on the floor propped up against the sofa watching some program, I don't remember what, on TV. Kathleen and I were just holding hands. We were so thrilled to be alone together that it didn't really matter what we did. Just sitting there shoulder to shoulder made my heart beat a little faster.

Her hand in mine was warm and soft, but I couldn't say that it was in any way relaxed. Actually, her fingertips were busy moving ever so softly in a very familiar circular motion deep in the palm of my hand. It was a special language of love between us that we had both learned to silently comprehend. The tips of her fingers could signal almost anything, but tonight the message was blazing desire.

As we were sitting there, her fingertips were becoming more insistent, but I teasingly pretended not to understand. With no immediate response from me, Kathleen feigned a pout and deliberately withdrew her hand. She sat there beside me like that for just a minute or two. Her sullen antics made me smile! Beautiful, perfect Kathleen was impersonating someone's dejected lover.

She couldn't stand our game for long though, and, frankly, neither could I. Moving around in front of me, she sat on her knees and captured my eyes with one of her riveting stares. Her amazing piercing green eyes were dancing to an urgent beat that would not be denied. She slipped both hands around my neck and pulled me to her. Just looking at Kathleen made me want her, but kissing her, even tenderly, ignited a frenzy of passion within me.

Quickly, the kissing turned insistent, and then almost instantly it was demanding. Our lovemaking was always spontaneous, passionate, and yes, I can also say that it was extremely vigorous. Tonight's lovemaking was no different. Our need for each other had been inflamed; now it raged like a wild fire. I can't tell you exactly how at the moment, but somehow we shed our clothes.

Kathleen lay stretched out on the floor face down on the carpet and I was on lying on top of her. I was kissing the back of her neck, the side of her face and the corner of her lips as she turned her head up to meet my lips. I took her hands in mine and slowly stretched our arms out wide so I could feel every beautiful inch of her fit, amazing body.

Our bodies were one, it seemed, as I brought our hands down to her side. Slowly, our fingers found their way under Kathleen's undulating groin. We both made glorious magical love to her until she whispered, "Yes, yes," and then, "Oh, yes." I felt her whole body tense, then shudder wonderfully for the longest time. Unable to move, we stayed that way until I finally regained enough strength to grab a throw from the sofa. We slept that way for a few minutes or maybe even an hour.

I realized, as I reflected on our last night together that just a touch, just a word from Kathleen in her right mind would mean everything to me right then. I didn't just like her; I adored her. I was convinced that she was the love of my life. She had to come back, and she had to come back to me. Waiting and not knowing what was going on was driving me crazy. Added to that, there was the sure knowledge that Joe Murray, Kathleen's brother-in-law, had outed us to the whole county.

Chapter 7

Paducah was the county seat of McCracken County, but the Bluegrass Motor Lodge, our little independent motel, was the seat of power and corruption for Paducah and that part of the state. Since I didn't work the night shift and I was only a woman, I wasn't privy to the shady and sometimes outright illegal activities that were going on using our little motel as a front. Without my knowledge, Scott, in spite of being the preacher's son, had involved himself with a group of low-level organized crime hoods out of Louisville.

With Scott's approval, these gangsters were running an illegal pinball machine operation out of our motel. While it was not against the law to have pinball machines, it was against the law to have them pay out. When they paid out, that was gambling, and gambling was definitely against the law in McCracken County. Many restaurants like ours had pinball machines, but there were also some bars and out of the way places that allowed them for gambling.

When they were doing something they didn't want their wives or neighbors to see, many of Scott's buddies including the Sheriff, the local head of the Highway Patrol, the City Building Superintendent, the county Judge, and the Mayor all made use of our motel rooms.

Scott scratched their backs, and they returned the favor. For example, when we were building our new motel and restaurant on the other side of town, so-called leftover city concrete worth many thousands of dollars was poured, free of charge, in the drainage conduits in front of the new motel.

Chapter 8

One day, I got a call from Bobbie over at the insurance office. She sounded nervous and said it was urgent; she wanted me to get over to her office right away. Since Bobbie was the only one in Paducah that knew about and supported Kathleen and me, my mind, of course, raced, wondering if her call had something to do with Kathleen.

I parked out front, like I usually did, when I got to her building. The receptionist immediately said to go on back, that Bobbie was expecting me. As I walked down the aisle to Bobbie's office, I heard voices talking. When I got close enough to the door to see in, I stalled mid-stride. I just stood there, my mouth agape. Finally, Bobbie asked, "Mandy, you remember Kathleen don't you?"

There was a woman sitting in a chair in front of Bobbie's desk, but this woman only faintly resembled Kathleen. She looked to be fifteen years older than Kathleen did the last time I saw her in my living room shortly before her father died. Her face was gaunt and vacant, her eyes were dull and lifeless, her body was frail, and her beautiful hair was pulled back in a severe bun. I had never seen her hair like that. It was awful. It was a long time before I could speak, but finally, I replied, "Yes, I remember Kathleen."

Bobbie said that Kathleen had been ill and wasn't driving yet, so her brother dropped her off for a visit while he ran errands for their farm. Bobbie asked Kathleen if she remembered me. At first, there was not even a glimmer of recognition, but then she indicated she thought she remembered me from church but she wasn't really sure. Kathleen told Bobbie and me that she was getting married the following month to a friend of the family's, a major in the army whose wife had died of ovarian cancer, leaving him with three kids.

I couldn't believe what I was hearing; Kathleen's words literally took my breath away. She was saying things that profoundly impacted my life, but the way she was saying them was like she was telling a casual acquaintance and not at all like she had been the love of my life.

I could not stand it any longer. Without saying another word, I turned around and somehow walked down the hall. I got in my car and collapsed, sobbing uncontrollably against the steering wheel. I literally went to pieces right out there in front of the insurance office.

From what I could tell, Kathleen had absolutely no memory of our relationship. When I looked into her eyes, I saw nothing of the person she had been to me. Evidently, whatever had happened to her had erased large parts of her memory. Kathleen had come back to some extent, but she had not come back to me.

All the long waiting and the ridicule I had endured had been for nothing. Kathleen's mother's word had ruled. Mary Crutchfield said that Kathleen would marry a man and now it was coming to pass. The woman I had seen in Bobbie's office was not my precious, beautiful Kathleen. Instead the person was just a shell of a woman, a puppet in her mother's hands.

I went back to the motel, went upstairs to the living quarters that I shared with my little boy, and laid across my bed. Feeling heartbroken and utterly alone, I didn't know which way to turn. Oh, Bobbie knew a little of what I was going through, but really there was no one who really understood what I had just lost. I was sick in the very depths of my soul. I no longer had even a shred of hope that Kathleen and I would ever be together again. The many months of waiting were over, and it had certainly not ended as I hoped it would.

Chapter 9

Hoping for reconciliation between Scott and me, Scott and his parents continued to press me to go to California to the Christian Counseling Center that advertised through the Southern Baptist Convention literature that it could cure people of homosexuality. All three of them took the stance that it was a horrible "disease" that could be cured if the patient really wanted to be free of the "illness."

To say that my life had crumbled after seeing Kathleen like that was a vast understatement. My world was literally smashed into tiny bits and pieces. At that point, I didn't see how I could go on, but I knew that I had to somehow for Patrick's sake. I was all he had, and, now, he was all I had. Regardless of how I felt, I knew that I had to pull myself together for him.

I told Scott that I was tired of living the way we were and I still wanted the divorce. Patrick and I would move to Lexington. The university was there and I wanted to finish my college education. Scott remained against the divorce, but finally said that if I would agree to go to the Christian Counseling Center out in California first, then, when I came back if I still wanted a divorce he would give me one and would also give me full custody of Patrick.

Under those terms, I agreed to go to California for the *homo treatment*, as I called it. My sister, Midget, and her husband, a marine, lived within an hour's distance of the Christian Counseling Center. Patrick and I went to stay with them while I paid weekly visits to the center. My sister and her husband knew that Scott and I were having trouble, so they thought I was out there for marital counseling. Neither of them had a clue that I was a lesbian.

The center assigned a male counselor to me. Although he was a trained, mainstream psychologist, he worked at the Christian center and was supposed to give treatment according to the Bible's teachings on homosexuality.

Mostly, we talked about my life and what I had recently endured. He explained to me that what happened to Kathleen was much like what happens to people in war; it was called PTSD. When her father died before her eyes while he was trying to hit her, it triggered the mental condition that she was experiencing. He said that Kathleen needed treatment as soon as possible. I seriously doubted that her family had taken her for treatment, and I had no legal right or any possible way now to interfere. She was twenty-seven years old and had forgotten who she really was.

The counselor quoted Bible verses about the forbidden sin, but I could tell from the way he was acting that he didn't seem to be all that convinced that living a lesbian or gay lifestyle was actually that bad. Maybe he worked there simply for the paycheck, I don't know, but he finally concluded, "If two people really love each other, I don't see anything wrong with them making a life together, even if it is two people of the same sex."

That was all I needed. I packed up little Patrick, told my sister and her husband goodbye, and my young son and I headed back to Paducah. When I got back, I told Scott that nothing had happened in California to change my mind. In fact, I wanted out of the marriage now more than ever. Patrick was two-and-a-half years old now; it had been more than a year since I told Scott I was a lesbian, and it had more than a year since he had beaten me.

It would probably have been much easier for everyone except me to go back to Scott, but after I met Kathleen, I realized that I had basically lived a lie and a passionless life. Though Scott had behaved very badly, if I hadn't found my true identity, I probably would have forgiven him and gone on to live my humdrum existence.

Through Kathleen, I discovered that I was a lesbian. In my heart, I knew that I could never really be happy living as a straight woman again. And as awful as Scott had been, he deserved a chance to find someone with whom he could truly be happy. I could not give him what he wanted. I was made to be with a woman, and I believed that woman for me was Kathleen, despite the tragic circumstances that caused her fragile mental state and ended our relationship.

Chapter 10

Scott finally agreed to the divorce and said that one of our lawyer friends could do the divorce papers for both of us since we had already agreed on the terms. Together, we sat down with J.C. Myers, a young attorney who we had known for several years. I knew both J.C. and his wife, Barb. They used to be part of our couples bowling league. J.C. was like a lot of small town attorneys, his practice consisted of a little bit of everything. He was handling some other legal matters for us related to the new motel and restaurant, so I wasn't expecting anything shady from him. In fact, while I definitely didn't trust Scott, it never occurred to me to not trust J.C.

As soon as J.C. had the rough draft of the divorce papers ready, he sent it over for me to approve. Everything was just as we had discussed when Scott and I were sitting in his office. When the final divorce papers were ready for us to sign, I dropped by J.C.'s office and signed on the line requiring my signature. All that was left was for Scott to sign them and the divorce would be in the works. Once the papers were filed, we had to wait 60 days.

Since neither of us was contesting anything, our divorce would be a simple one. We would split everything down the middle. It was customary during the late 1960s for the mother to get custody of her children, so I was to have full custody of Patrick. You couldn't get much simpler than that, or so I thought anyway.

By that time our new motel and restaurant on the other side of town was almost finished, I agreed to help Scott get it opened while we were waiting for the 60 days to pass.

I continued managing the old motel, helped get the new motel and restaurant open, and started thinking about what I would do when Patrick and I were finally free

Scott and I still owned our home, the home we lived in prior to moving to the Blue Grass living quarters. That would have to be sold. We owned a hundred-acre tree farm a few miles out of town that was worth a substantial sum since it was paid for. We owned a half-interest in the new motel and restaurant, and a half-interest in a housing subdivision behind the new motel and restaurant. We had done very well in Paducah, in spite of all our marital problems.

Scott was acting surprisingly amiable about finalizing the divorce settlement. He even agreed to buy me out so I would have enough money to live while I finished my education at the University of Kentucky in Lexington. Although Scott had been acting like an angel, I still refused to let my guard down, but I reasoned that since Scott wanted to make his home in Paducah, it would be in his best interest to buy me out rather than for us to have to sell everything and split the proceeds down the middle.

While I was in California for the *homo treatment*, my mother, Faith Ann, finally divorced her sorry husband. My sister, Vickie, got married and moved away. Nita, my sixteen-year-old youngest sister moved to Tennessee with her father. When I got back from California, mother had an empty nest. She didn't know what to do with herself.

After my divorce was final, the plan was for mother to move with me to Lexington and take care of Patrick while I was in school. Everything was falling into place it seemed for me to finally be free and for Patrick, mother, and I to start over with a new life.

For the first time in a long time, while I wasn't happy, I was feeling a little optimistic. I just hoped Scott would live up to his agreement, but under the terms of the divorce papers I had signed, I didn't see how he could avoid doing what the divorce decree stipulated. The last thing I needed was any more trouble, so, yes, at this time, I was very hopeful.

I reconciled myself to the knowledge that Kathleen was gone from me. She had married and moved with her new husband and his three kids to somewhere in Texas. I often wondered if her mind ever returned to her true self or if she ever thought of us. What would she think or do if she ever regained her senses and all of her memory?

Some might say Kathleen's pass at me more than two years ago had destroyed both our lives, but in spite of all the horrible things that had happened, including the physical abuse, I knew that Kathleen had handed me the keys that had unlocked the door to my real identity. For that, as strange as it may sound, I was grateful.

As the time got closer to the date when the divorce would be final, mother and I went to Lexington to find an apartment. Not knowing for sure how things would go, we got a six-month lease on a really cute three-bedroom townhouse not too far from the University. Little-by-little, we moved some of our things over there.

I wanted a new living room suite, but the bedroom furniture would be what we already had. We were beginning to get really excited about our new life in Lexington.

Chapter 11

Late in the afternoon, the day before I thought the divorce was to be final, Scott told me that I needed to go down to the old courthouse to pick up some property settlement papers at the County Judge's office. He said it casually like you might say, "Pick up some barbecue for dinner." We were building the new motel and restaurant, so it wasn't unusual for me to pick up permit papers of one kind or another, and that was the tone Scott used that day. His voice and manner indicated that the errand was like so many other ordinary ones I'd run before.

Scott said that the papers had to be signed before a notary and that they had to be executed before the divorce could be finalized. He said that his mom and dad would take care of Patrick while I was at the courthouse. At the time, I thought that was a little strange because Polly didn't enjoy being around small children, including her grandson, Patrick. But, still, I didn't think too much about it. I just wanted to get it done, pick up Patrick, and go home for the day.

When I got to the old courthouse, I parked my car and walked up the steps just like I had done many times in the past, but as I got inside the courthouse door, a deputy sheriff approached me. He had some folded papers in his hand. As he got closer to me, he asked me if I were Amanda Carol Blackwood Allen; I was taken aback, but answered that I was. He opened the papers and started reading to me in a loud voice in the middle of the ancient courthouse floor.

While I don't remember what he said word for word, some of the terms he used are forever burned in my brain. He read that temporary primary custody of Patrick had been awarded to Scott, and that I had been declared an *unfit mother*.

The deputy closed the papers and roughly forced them into my hands. Instantly, I knew that I had been double-crossed and that Scott and his parents had conspired to take Patrick from me. I also realized that the divorce papers I had signed giving me full custody of Patrick and splitting everything down the middle had never been filed. Wild with fear, I drove the few minutes to Scott's parent's house. They claimed that Scott had come for Patrick and they didn't know where he was.

Maybe they knew or maybe they didn't, but from then on I never trusted either one of them again — even Brother Allen, despite his initial help of me. From their house, I drove to the new restaurant where Scott was supposed to be. When he saw me, he was, at first, afraid that I would attack him on the spot and in public. But then he remembered the considerable leverage he had on me. He regained his composure and calmly told me that if I ever wanted to see Patrick again, I would have to agree to his terms of the settlement, custody, and divorce.

We walked to the private office of our new motel where Scott unveiled for the first time an entirely different set of divorce papers he wanted me to sign; papers I'd never seen before. At first, I was furious at J.C., but then I could tell from the cover letterhead that these papers had been drawn up by an entirely different law firm and not by J.C. Scott had apparently never signed the ones I'd signed; he had never intended for those papers to be filed.

He was stringing me along those 60 days hoping that I would change my mind I guess. I'd been completely duped. According to this new set of papers, Scott was to have primary custody of Patrick, he was to keep all of our assets, and I would leave with nothing. As long as I agreed not to live with a woman, I could keep Patrick in Lexington with my mother. That was it; I could take it or leave it.

Furious, I told him that I would get a lawyer and fight him. He laughed sarcastically and said for me to try if I could. I walked out of the motel office, went home, and started right then to systematically call every attorney in the county. I told each one of them my story, but no one would take my case, not even J.C. The good-old-boy system was operating in full swing in McCracken County. Either Scott had them in the palm of his hand, or he had done favors for someone in power over them.

They were all a bunch of gutless cowards. This was 1967. They did not want to be involved in a messy, and what would be a notorious, case involving a lesbian fighting for her rights and the custody of her child.

How, in our country, can a mother lose custody of her child without ever having seen a lawyer or without ever going before a judge? How can a woman be declared unfit based on someone else's word? While I had admitted to Scott privately that Kathleen and I loved each other, there was absolutely no proof that could be brought against me. There had never been a custody hearing. Kathleen was now married and had moved to Texas. It was preposterous, yet it was happening. Custody of my child was legally being taken from me.

Apparently, after I had returned from California and Scott knew that my mind was made up about the divorce, Scott had persuaded his friend, the county Judge, to issue the custody decree based on nothing but his word that I was an unfit mother.

Scott didn't want or love Patrick. In fact, although Patrick was almost three years old now, he barely knew him. Scott's long-standing vendetta against me had come to this. I wouldn't do what he wanted, so he would use his crooked connections to destroy me. He wanted to punish me for taking his home from him, but most of all he wanted to punish me for emasculating him in front of all his friends.

Chapter 12

That same night, Patrick pitched such a fit to be with his mommy that Scott brought him to me. I was never so glad to see anyone in my entire life, as I was to see my precious little boy. Patrick had been crying and so had I. When I saw him I was still crying. Just being able to hold him in my arms gave me hope. There just had to be a way to break the stranglehold Scott had on me. He had apparently never intended to keep Patrick. The whole cruel ploy was a scare tactic to bring me in line and keep me under his thumb.

While Scott was standing there in the doorway of our living quarters, he again told me that he would allow me to move to Lexington with my mother. I could keep Patrick, but he would retain primary custody, and the divorce would be under his terms. In addition, I would lose everything financially, and, as long as Patrick lived with me, I could not live with a woman.

He was looking at me as if he had, at long last, paid me back. Neither Scott nor any of his crooked friends took into account that he had totally ignored Patrick and me for many months before I ever started seeing Kathleen.

Even so, in the eyes of the community because I was a lesbian, I didn't deserve basic human consideration. And in spite of the fact that Scott and his family were staunch Christians, they felt justified in doing what they were doing to me. After all, I was a lesbian and I deserved losing everything, including custody of my son.

I'll never forget, it was summertime when the three of us pulled out of Paducah heading to our townhouse in Lexington. In spite of all the painful waiting and the recent trauma, I felt a little lighter with every mile. As long as I had Patrick, I would find a way to get my college education, and I would find a way to keep my son.

Scott thought he had beaten me, but all he had really done was make me stronger. It felt good to know that I was being true to myself. While I could have pretended to be cured from homosexuality, I couldn't stomach the whole idea. In the end, I didn't leave Scott and Paducah to be with Kathleen, the woman I thought was the love of my life, I left for the opportunity to be myself, which happened to include being a lesbian.

As soon as we got to Lexington, I started looking for a job. There would be no savings and no settlement. And I no longer had a car. Scott, in a final attempt to break my spirit, had also taken my car as one of the assets of the marriage. Thankfully, we had mother's car, an older black VW bug, which we nicknamed "Blackie."

I tried to get a student loan for college, but the financial aid officer at the university said that I didn't qualify for a loan since I had been married. When I told them that I had a child, and that I needed the money more than anyone did, they looked at me as if I were nuts. Women with children, in their opinion, should stay at home and take care of them. I would have to support the three of us and go to college, but that I was more than willing to do. With each new adversity, I grew more determined to provide for Patrick and make a happy life for all of us.

My mother, Faith Ann, still didn't know that I was a lesbian; she thought I was leaving Scott because he had been running around on me for years. As the manager of our restaurant, she had the opportunity to hear all the gossip around the restaurant and motel, and she had heard from some of our cooks and waitresses that Scott had been sleeping around on me ever since we brought little Patrick home from the adoption center. I had naively believed that he was attending Masonic meetings and going fishing all those nights. As it turned out, Scott had been the one to break our marriage vows long before I ever thought of being in a relationship with Kathleen.

So, during the time he was treating Patrick and me as if we didn't exist, he had also been having sex with other women and even had steady girlfriends. It was common knowledge around town, and everyone knew but me.

It has always been more than interesting to me that a married man can commit adultery, beat his wife, treat his wife and child like dirt, and be involved in illegal activities, but to Christian society, he is still much better than any lesbian is. The mere fact that I had loved a woman made it okay for Scott and our crooked legal system in McCracken County to strip everything I had away from me.

I got a job working in a factory at night so I could go to school in the daytime. Mother kept Patrick for me and we started to settle down into a peaceful routine. Patrick, mother, and I were all a lot happier now that we had gotten away from all the stress that had been happening back in Paducah.

Chapter 13

Within a couple of months, however, we started to see Scott's red truck parked out in the parking lot of our townhouse community. From what my mother said, Scott had been watching our home and had also been watching me when I left to go to work or to school. I had no idea what he was up to. The divorce laid out by Scott still hadn't gone through yet, but as the terms of his divorce papers stipulated, I had left with nothing financially. I wasn't living with a woman. What more could Scott want?

The following Friday night as I was walking over to Blackie, I saw his truck again. I started walking toward it. Scott started his truck and actually tried to run me over. I ran back to Blackie, jumped in, and started to pull out of the parking lot. Scott ran Blackie, with me in it, off the road into a ditch and then started laughing. I was sure then that he had completely lost his mind. I didn't know what to do, but I knew for certain that I was in danger, and I also knew that I had to get Patrick, mother, and me away from there and to safety.

The next evening when I was at work, Scott paid a visit to Patrick and mother. He told mother that he was surprised that I had been able to find a job and was going to be able to make it without him. It seemed that he had taken everything expecting me to come crawling back since he thought I would have no way to support the three of us.

Then he made a threat to my mother that would prove to be his biggest mistake. He told mother that he was going to send Patrick back to the State of Kentucky on the grounds that we had gotten him under false pretenses.

From all the mean and hateful things he had already done, I had no reason to believe that he wouldn't do it. Regardless, now I knew positively that Scott could not be trusted to keep his word on any front. Being thwarted in his plan, he was now trying to terrify me in any way he could. It was plain that he was determined to do whatever it took to force us back home to Paducah.

Scott had grossly underestimated me. In fact, all his efforts to scare us were actually working against him. After everything that we had been through, I was determined more than ever to not let Scott drag us back. We were away from him now, and that was how we would continue to be if I had anything to do with it.

Legally, Scott had underhandedly gained temporary primary custody of Patrick. However, at the time, it was not considered criminal parental kidnapping if either one of the parents took the child across the state line. It was, instead, considered a misdemeanor in the state of Kentucky, which meant next to nothing once you crossed the state line. Knowing that, I hatched a plan to move Patrick and me out of the state of Kentucky. I had to get us away from McCracken County where Scott had so much power with the local authorities, and where I couldn't even get a lawyer to take my case to do so much as to mount a custody hearing.

First, since Scott had been patrolling the parking lot of our townhouse in Lexington, I knew I had to be careful. Late that same night after Scott threatened my mother to send Patrick back to the state, I put mother and Patrick on a Greyhound bus to my sister, Midget's, in Beaufort, South Carolina. In the time since I'd stayed with them for the *homo treatment*, they had been transferred from the base in California to Beaufort, South Carolina.

Mother's VW bug, old Blackie, would still be in the parking lot, and I would keep the lights on in the townhouse so it would look like someone was home. Even if Scott policed the lot five times a day, he wouldn't suspect anything.

Mother would immediately return to Lexington once I had my escape plans finalized. That way, to all appearances, it would look like we were still at the townhouse in Lexington. We hoped it would be a few days, or maybe even a week or longer, until Scott figured out that while mother was still in the townhouse, Patrick and I were long gone.

There were still a few more months left on our lease on the Lexington townhouse. Without question, my decision to take Patrick and go on the run left everything in all of our lives in a major uproar. At the time, we didn't know what all the fallout would be for any of us. For Christ's sake, I'd never broken the law before. I don't think I had even had a parking ticket; this was an entirely new game to me.

Mother didn't know what she would eventually do, but for those few months that were left on the lease, at least, she would be living at the townhouse. That would give her time to decide what she really wanted to do. With her divorce final and all of her girls gone, she was as free as a bird for the first time in years, to hear her tell it.

Mother, bless her heart, repeatedly told me not to worry about her. She lectured, "I have a little money saved. Take care of Patrick and yourself, Mandy, I can either get a job here in Lexington or move to Beaufort where your sister is." I felt terrible that all of our wonderful plans had been disrupted by Scott's crazy, and, what I felt was dangerous behavior, but both mother and I agreed it wasn't safe for Patrick and me to continue to stay in Lexington any longer.

Taking Patrick across the state line was drastic, but Scott had simply left me no choice. There was no way that my son was going to be sent back to the state if I could help it.

Through generous lesbian friends, I found a place in St. Paul, Minnesota for Patrick and me to live. I took the Greyhound to Beaufort, and the two of us flew to Minnesota where I would find a job to support us. Mother headed back to Lexington.

Of course, Scott would be furious when he found out. He would, no doubt, be relentless in his efforts to find us, but though I was terrified, I realistically didn't see how he could track us down. I had been careful to leave no trail, and besides that, I had the able help of the unofficial lesbian underground, a group of lesbians across the country who were committed to helping lesbian mothers keep their children. I felt like we would be safe, at least, until I could figure out something more permanent for us.

Mandy Episode 4

Chapter 1

The sharp piano wire came whipping and singing down what looked like a long, round, metal overhead laundry chute. As the rookie employee in the section, my job consisted of grabbing the end of the lashing wire and feeding it onto a big, wooden spool where it would be rolled up, stored, and eventually shipped to different piano manufacturing plants all over the world.

My supervisor, a huge, unkempt woman with wild washed-out reddish hair and a few broken tobacco stained teeth, wore filthy blue-bibbed overalls and black steel-toed work boots. She and the other vulgar talking women in our section laughed hysterically as I tried my best to wrangle the end of the wire and attach it to the waiting spool.

By the end of my first day, nearly all my nails were broken and the palms of both hands were bleeding through the thin, cloth gloves they gave us to wear. "Don't worry young lady, if you last that long, in a couple of weeks you will build up enough hard calluses on those little soft hands of yours that you won't feel a thing!" The mocking supervisor said.

I had taken the first job I could find after my son, Patrick, and I had gotten to St. Paul, Minnesota, but in spite of my urgent need to support my young son and myself, I made a firm vow after that first demoralizing day that I would find a better, if not a higher paying job, as soon as I possibly could.

After all, I did have some training and also some experience as a legal secretary. I'd been to secretarial school, could type at least seventy-five words per minute, and was pretty fast at taking shorthand. I wasn't a whiz or anything, but I knew my skills were more than adequate for most secretarial jobs. Unfortunately, a job needing my qualifications and experience wasn't ready and waiting like this one was at the piano wire factory, and I had rent to pay and groceries to buy right away.

My plan was to stick with the factory only until I could find something better. I had no intentions of ending up in the bottom of what could have easily passed for a big, empty coal bin the rest of my working days.

Actually, until I found myself in the midst of the coarse, sneering, straight women at the piano wire factory, the women I'd met in St. Paul had all been extremely kind to Patrick and me. Erin Abernathy, the amazingly kind woman I shared a townhouse with, picked us up from the airport, drove us to our new home, fed us a wonderful home-cooked meal, and put us to bed in our lovely, clean bedroom.

Erin had a smile as big as the one you saw on those yellow smiley faces, short graying blond hair, wide pale blue eyes, a stocky build, and was neatly dressed in blue slacks and a yellow, button-down cotton shirt. When we stepped off the plane in St. Paul, she was holding a small white sign that said, *Welcome Patrick and Mandy*. I liked her instantly and was relieved to know that we were not only safe, but also in good hands. Erin treated us as if we were honored guests. There has to be a special place reserved in heaven for Erin and people like her. She was literally a lifesaver for Patrick and me.

Two of Erin's friends took us all out to dinner the next evening. We also met a lesbian couple who had children around Patrick's age who lived in the same townhouse complex that we did. Their situation was very similar to mine; they were basically hiding from an ex-husband who was trying to take the two kids because he had found out their mother was a lesbian. My husband, Scott, had beaten me, tried to kill me, and threatened to send Patrick back to the state when I told him I was a lesbian in love with Kathleen Crutchfield.

Scott told Kathleen's father to keep her away from me the night I confessed my love of her. Her father had a fatal heart attack over hearing Kathleen was a lesbian and died right in front of her. Kathleen suffered some sort of a mental breakdown, forgot who I was, and that we had ever loved each other.

In order to save face in the community, her mother, a closeted lesbian herself, forced Kathleen to marry an Army officer with a bunch of kids. Kathleen, her new husband, and the flock moved to Texas … and that was that.

That was that, except now I had a wonderful little boy to bring up alone, and the woman I loved had been erased from my life as though she never existed. This had to be secondary, however, to Patrick's needs. His birth mother, a young teenager, had given him up for adoption immediately; I had made him a promise to love him, take care of him, and never leave him, and I intended, with everything in me, to keep my word.

Erin worked as a Nurse Anesthetist for St. Joseph's Hospital and was part of an unofficial underground lesbian network who helped mothers on the run from their husbands, ex-husbands, or even the law, if need be. When some lesbian friends in Louisville had contacted Erin about my situation, she offered to let Patrick and I move in with her and rent a room until we could get on our feet.

Chapter 2

So, I ran. I had been exposed to what real love was real for me. Love filled with care, tenderness, and passion. I could never go back to a life with Scott or any other man. In retrospect, it would have been far easier for me to fake it with Scott until Patrick was older, but the whole idea of being intimate with a man was revolting to me after being with Kathleen. I didn't know whether I would ever find love again, but I did know that I had to be true to myself, a lesbian.

After I ran to St. Paul, Scott was harassing my mother, who still lived in the Lexington, Kentucky townhouse that Patrick and I had shared with her. He was pestering the life out of her trying to find out where Patrick and I were. She told him she didn't know anymore than he did, but he kept hounding her and threatening to bring in the police.

Mother and I both knew there wasn't really anything he could do legally, as it wasn't against the law to take your own child across state lines in 1967, even if the other parent did have temporary primary custody.

Though the law did change later, at that time his threats were really more of a nuisance than anything else. In the weeks after Patrick and I left, I felt terrible that my mother was the one having to put up with Scott's insane jealous antics, but there wasn't anything we could do about it until she could vacate the townhome we had shared.

In the meantime, mother and I had set up a way to communicate through Violet, a terrific friend of ours who also lived in Lexington. Violet had never been married, but she was always unashamedly on the hunt for a man. Mother and I teased her about it all the time. Violet used to work as a waitress at the restaurant in Paducah but moved to Lexington to go back to college to become a social worker.

Violet knew about Scott's fooling around on me, but she didn't know that I was a lesbian. Honestly, I don't think it would have mattered to her one bit even if she had found out. She was just one of those really good people who would do anything for you if she liked you, but also wouldn't go out of her way to say anything bad about you if you weren't on the top of her list of favorites. In other words, Violet wasn't a gossip. In my experience, the world could sure use more people like her.

Not only did Violet have a heart of gold, but she was also the most liberal person I'd ever met. It didn't matter to her what color your skin was or how much money you had; she treated everyone equally. Violet had the rare ability to look past the exterior straight into the innermost part of anyone's soul. Because she was intensely honest, most people were uncomfortable around her, but mother, Patrick, and I just loved her and looked forward to her spur-of-the-minute visits and the outings.

Violet would sometimes show up at our townhouse on the weekends and wake us all up with a sack full of sausage and egg biscuits. She wanted all three of us to get dressed and go out to Lake Barkley with her, but usually mother would beg off. So off we would go, Patrick, Violet, and me. We would take Patrick down to the wading area and then when he tired of that, we would rent a boat, fish a little, or just go tour around the lake.

Because she was such a trusted friend, I would mail my letters to mother in care of Violet and she would mail her letters to me from the post office. There was no correspondence to or from me that could be traced to my mother's Lexington townhouse address. We suspected that Scott might be policing her mailbox and didn't want to take any chances.

Additionally, on Friday nights at 6:30 p.m., I would call Violet where mother would be waiting. Mother would bring me up to speed on what an ass Scott was being and the news of the rest of family, and I would tell her the latest of our adventures in St. Paul. Of course, once mother moved from our old townhouse, we would have to make different communication arrangements so Scott still couldn't find me, but for the immediate future this plan would do.

Chapter 3

A few weeks into my job at the piano wire factory, Erin told me about a job opening for a clerk in the Director of Purchasing Department at the hospital. I had kept the books for Scott's and my motel and restaurant business back in our hometown of Paducah, and I had a memory like an elephant for numbers, so I applied for the job, which paid nearly what I was making at the piano wire factory.

When St. Joseph's HR called me in for the interview, I was thrilled but pretty nervous. God how I hated my job at the factory, and although I didn't really hate the women I worked with, I can honestly say that I would have been more than glad if I never had to lay eyes on the factory or any of my coworkers again.

Human Resources interviewed quite a number of people for the job, which requirements were really just using common sense and following simple directions. My typing skills would come in handy, but mostly, you just worked with the accounting work sheets. They selected only three applicants to meet with the Purchasing Director.

The morning I met with Jordan McCall, the Purchasing Director, she was intently bent over a work sheet that was almost as wide as her desk. When she looked up to greet me, her eyes were penetrating and powerful, but she seemed to be genuinely interested in me as a person and not just as a potential employee. I told her my story as honestly as I could, leaving out the part about being on the run with my son. I told her about Patrick, of course; I just didn't tell her we were hiding from my husband.

As she stood to indicate that our meeting was over, I noticed for the first time how attractive she was. I guessed her to be in her early forties, slim and tall with her dark auburn hair pulled back in a bun at the nape of her neck. Her eyes were the color of flint, with a few tiny shards of what looked like sparkling glass glinting here and there. Her complexion was a light olive, the kind most women would kill for. Smartly dressed in a light gray suit and simple black pumps and sure of herself, she showed me to the door and said that she had enjoyed meeting me.

As I left her office, I smiled a little to myself, aware of the fact that it was the first time since Kathleen that I had noticed another woman was attractive.

To my amazement, the next day after the interview with Jordan McCall, St. Joseph's called and said I had the job. Erin gave me the news when I got in from the factory. We danced joyously around the room. It was a Friday night. We got a sitter for Patrick, called the rest of the gang, went out to dinner, and then to a place called "The Townhouse," a gay and lesbian bar, to celebrate.

It was the first time since Patrick and I had arrived in St. Paul that I really felt like we were going to have a way to make it on our own. It wouldn't be easy, but like millions of other working, single mothers, I would be able to provide for my child.

We had all been dancing, laughing, and celebrating my good fortune that night. The place was packed, but we were having our own little party in a back corner booth. We were not paying too much attention to the rest of the crowd when suddenly I felt an almost imperceptible tap on my left shoulder, "Amanda Carol Allen, I believe?"

For a moment I sat, unable to move in my seat, immediately thinking that somehow Scott had found me. No one, other than my mother, ever called me anything other than Mandy, so I was shocked to hear someone call me by my full legal name. As I turned to get a better look at the person with the soft, unknown voice, she asked. "Would you like to dance?" There she was, the tall woman with flint-tinted eyes, Jordan McCall, with her flowing, auburn hair falling down around her shoulders asking me to dance.

Erin and my friends were mischievously grinning at me as I got up and took her outstretched hand. Of course, at the time, they didn't know she was my new boss or they might not have been so elated. Skillfully, she led me around the dance floor away from my friends. Then she said, "You could have knocked me over with a feather when I noticed you sitting you over there. I thought it might be awkward if you suddenly recognized me, so I thought I would just make the first move. Today is my birthday and my friends and I are celebrating."

I replied, "Well, congratulations and Happy Birthday, Jordan. I have to say that I'm more than a little surprised to see you here, too. My friends and I are celebrating my new job that I start in two weeks."

Obviously amused, her dark charcoal eyes with the bluish shards twinkled as she teased, "Oh! And would that be the job working in my department at St. Joseph's?"

"One and the same," I smiled up into her grinning face.

She expertly kept up the rhythm of the song, "I let HR know that you were my pick, but they don't always hire the person I recommend. Sometimes I wonder why they even send people over for me to interview. But I must tell you Amanda, you made quite an impression on me and it wasn't just for your bookkeeping experience and typing skills either."

When I realized she was flirting with me, I was sure my face was flushing seventeen shades of red. Though Jordan was extremely attractive, she was at least fifteen years my senior. Not that age would matter if you were really in love with someone, but my heart wasn't ready for any sort of romantic relationship. My focus was strictly on taking care of Patrick and giving us both a stable home.

We danced through a couple of songs and on the way back to my friends, Jordan sighed, "You know, of course, that if anyone at work found out that we were lesbians that would be the end of our jobs."

Flustered, I said. "Don't worry; they won't hear a peep out of me." Silently, I was thinking, *I just hope to God that this doesn't cost me the job.*

Jordan called me the next night. She had copied my number from my personnel file. And, she called me every night thereafter. I asked her over to meet Erin and Patrick and, eventually, she found out the whole story about us being on the run.

At work, Jordan treated me as she did everyone else in the department; after work, it was an entirely different story. Within just a few weeks, she wanted Patrick and me to move in with her; she said she wanted to take care of us, and she also wanted us to be more than just friends. Wow, I'd only just met her! It was all moving way too fast for me and while I really liked Jordan, I didn't love her in the same way that she loved me.

Jordan and I dated and spent quite a bit of time together. All my friends were crazy about her, and I liked her friends, too. There were lots of parties at one home or the other, and we had a terrific time; but, it just was never going to be like the love Kathleen and I had shared. It was fun and I can't say that I wasn't flattered by her attention, but I just couldn't give Jordan what she wanted. Jordan wasn't a quitter though; she said she would wait for as long as it took for me to change my mind.

All in all, St. Paul had been good for Patrick and me. We had found a wonderful sitter for him in the same complex where we lived. He loved playing with the sitter's three kids, and on the weekends Jordan and I would take him to the park, to a movie, or on a picnic. Jordan had never been around any little ones, so interacting with children was new to her. She took to it like a duck to water, though, and would push him on the swings, ride the merry-go-round with him, or the three of us would play catch.

Chapter 4

Even though it had been only a few short months, Patrick and I were making a good life in St. Paul. It was, of course, difficult having to communicate with my mother the way I did, but other than that, we enjoyed a normal life. It was normal that is until my mother, on one of our Friday night chats, told me that the kidnapping laws had been changed in the State of Kentucky. And with the new legislation, it was now against the law for a parent who didn't have legal custody of the child to cross the state line. We were devastated by the news.

This meant that the FBI considered my taking Patrick to St. Paul to be criminal parental kidnapping, which was a federal offense. We knew that it would only be a matter of time before they found me through my Social Security work records. Afraid to stay any longer, I would have to quit my job and move with Patrick immediately.

Erin quickly went to bat for us. She called one of the members of the underground network in Lubbock, Texas. Again we found a savior in a wonderful older lesbian who agreed to take Patrick and me in. She offered safety and shelter to us, even though she knew that we were trying to avoid being found by federal agents.

To avoid leaving a trail for the authorities, Jordan took off work and drove us south to Donna Barbara Anna Foster's home on the outskirts of Lubbock. Although we didn't arrive until late in the evening, she was waiting for us with open arms. We would be safe with her, she said, until we could figure out what to do.

Patrick, Jordan, and I all cried when Jordan left the next day to drive the long way back to St. Paul. Jordan hesitated as she was getting in her car to leave, "You know, Mandy, you can still change your mind, come back to St. Paul and move in with me. I can provide for us and you won't have to work."

"Jordan, you know I can't do that. I have to work to support us; I just can't work too long at the same job. We'll be fine, don't worry." With that, and with tears streaming down both our faces, she pulled out of Donna's drive. That was the last time I ever saw Jordan, but I often remember her for being the wonderful person she was. She was beautiful, caring, kind, and she loved both Patrick and me and was willing to take care of us in spite of the obvious danger.

She would have done anything to make us happy — maybe under different circumstances it could have worked out given time, but not with me now being a fugitive from the FBI. The truth was I couldn't focus on a relationship if I had wanted to; all I could think about was getting away from St. Paul and keeping my baby and me safe.

Chapter 5

Donna Foster was quite a character. A retired military nurse, she had shared twenty-five years with a woman, a physical therapist, who had left her a couple of years back for someone "younger and sexier," as Donna in her characteristically frank and funny way had put it.

Donna had cancer, but you would never have known it. Lively and feisty for a sixty-year-old, she stayed active bowling, cooking, and gardening, but her favorite activity was golf. Oh Lord, did that plump little woman ever love golf. On Sundays, when I wasn't working as a checker at the local grocery store down the street, she, her friends, and I, played eighteen holes while Patrick rode in the golf cart.

If Donna had a fault, it was that she was a fiercely competitive golfer. She could not stand the thought of losing. She tended to cheat, especially when she had a bad lie in the rough, in the sand, in the fairway, or anywhere else for that matter. She would try to get between her ball and us and slyly move it to a better position without giving herself away. Her maneuvering antics were so predictable that we watched her like hawks to prevent her from fudging the ball.

The group had a standing rule that we would try not to let Donna get her hands on the scorecard, though she would fight for it every time. She was pretty good at writing our correct scores down but somehow her sevens, eights, and nines would all end up being fives. It was hysterically funny to all of us, but not to Donna; she was dead serious about her golf game. Unfortunately, Donna's game was nothing to brag about, so for about thirty minutes after we finished the last hole and the scores were tallied, she would pout and not speak to any of us.

As far as Patrick and I were concerned, though, she loved us as if we were her own. She had never had kids, her parents had long been dead, and she was an only child. That was the reason for her extra long name. She had been named after her aunts on both sides of her family.

Donna's big, old, sprawling, ranch-style house was unique for the time. As was common in the west Texas area in the late

1960s, the main floor of the ranch house had four bedrooms, three baths, a living room, dining room, and family room. Patrick and I had our own rooms, which was really wonderful. But what made the home so different was the small kitchen elevator lined with bright lavender, paisley wallpaper that went from the main floor to the basement. The entire basement was a huge party room lined all around with cushion-covered-built-in bench seats. The cushions were all covered in fabric that was exactly the same color and pattern as the wallpaper in the elevator.

Posters from all the top music artists of the day, and also the past twenty-five years, covered the knotted-pine walls. In the middle of the room was a shiny hardwood dance floor, and in one corner there was a silver custom DJ booth complete with every record imaginable. Donna collected records like some people collected rocks; she had to have at least one of everything that hit the charts.

Every so often she would throw a party down there and it wasn't unusual to have fifty lesbians dancing their legs off at any given time. I had started back to school at Texas Tech thinking that I could get at least one semester and a few classes in before we had to move again, so I had a few lesbian friends from the university to invite to the parties, but Donna, it seemed, knew every lesbian in Texas and half of New Mexico.

Chapter 6

At one of the parties, I noticed someone who I hadn't seen since Patrick and I had left Paducah to move to Lexington. So much had happened to us since I'd seen her that it took me a minute to place her, but then it all came rushing back.

I had met her with my sister. It was back when my younger sister, Amber, or as all the family called her, Midget, was driving with her college roommate, Robin, across the country to somewhere up in New Hampshire where Robin had a teaching job lined up for the next year. They had planned to stay with me a couple nights on their way.

I had never met Robin before, but I had heard a lot about her from Midget. She was tall, athletic (she had been a basketball player in college), about five-foot ten or so with hazel eyes and short brown wavy hair. She certainly wasn't beautiful like Kathleen or Jordan, but her quick wit, big heart, and ability to make anyone feel special drew people to her like a magnet.

From the first second she stepped out of my sister's little red VW bug, there was some sort of instant connection between us. *Good Lord!* I had thought. *Is my sister a lesbian, too?* But, no, that wasn't it. The truth was that Robin did indeed find herself attracted to me. But the problem was, as far as both my sister and Robin knew I was a happily married woman and a mother with a toddler.

I sensed Robin was embarrassed and confused about what she felt was a forbidden attraction to a married woman, and, to make matters worse, her best friend's sister. She probably had visions of my sister killing her. But since I already knew that I was a lesbian, planning a separation from Scott, and only waiting for my divorce to be final, I thought the whole darn situation was impossibly funny and decided to see how much I could make Robin squirm.

Later on the night that they arrived, while my sister was taking a shower, I asked Robin if she wanted to drive with me to get some ice cream. She was as nervous as anyone I'd ever seen, but she reluctantly agreed to go with me. While we were out, I outright accused her of her obvious attraction to a married woman with a baby. Robin turned red in the face and became instantly flustered. For a second, I thought she was going to bolt out of my car.

Finally, I couldn't contain my laughter a second longer and also out of mercy for her, I told her the truth about me, about my planned separation from Scott, and about my impending divorce. Just to put her at ease, I also told her the attraction was mutual.

Poor Robin was visibly relieved about the news but wondered why Midget didn't know that Scott and I were getting a divorce. I told her that I didn't want to spoil Midget's vacation and that I would call and tell her later. Midget didn't know that Robin was a lesbian even though they had shared a suite -- they had separate rooms, but shared a bath together -- when they were in college.

While Robin and I were definitely attracted to each other, she was going to New Hampshire and I was moving to Lexington, so we said we would write, which we never did, and, as far as we knew then, that was the end of it.

When I walked up to her at Donna's party, I said. "It's a small world isn't it." Robin's face lit up like a Christmas tree when she recognized me. She was fairly beaming; I could tell that she was really happy to see me again. After one year teaching in New Hampshire, she was back working on her master's at her old alma mater just across the state line from Lubbock in New Mexico. She came back to get her advanced degree there, because once you had your BS, it only took one more year to get the master's. Had she gone to a different university, it might have taken much longer.

The mutual attraction of two years ago was still there and we talked, laughed, and danced until the early hours of the morning.

Robin was single and lived in student housing near her university, which was only a couple of hours west of Lubbock. Robin started driving over to visit us on the weekends when she could, and we eventually became very close.

When you're on the run as I was, it is hard to keep remembering that you are doing the right thing. Robin knew that I was a good mother and she also knew that Scott didn't really want Patrick. He was just using his legal power to try to take Patrick away from me. I guess you could say that regardless of how difficult the road ahead seemed to be, Robin kept encouraging me to believe in myself. There were times when I felt anger and frustration over the injustice of a law that forced me to keep running. In those times,

Robin helped me to continue to believe in the rightness of what I was doing.

Robin and Patrick were crazy about each other. On the weekends when she was visiting, she would get up early on Sunday's so they could read the funny papers together while Donna and I fixed blueberry pancakes for us all. Some weekends Patrick, Robin, and I would go camping. We'd leave on Friday afternoon and drive back on Sunday in time for Robin to drive the two hours back to her school.

Chapter 7

One Sunday, as we got closer to Donna's house, there was a sea of cars parked all around the house and up and down both sides of the long driveway. Instinctively, I knew something was terribly wrong. At first, I thought it might have to do with Patrick and me, but then I started to recognize a lot of the cars. There were more vehicles there than for one of her famous parties. We had to park a long way from the house, but when we finally made it to the top of the driveway, someone told us that Donna had been found dead.

That simply can't be, I thought. We had just left her on Friday and she seemed fine. She had been laughing and joking with us as she walked us out to Robin's car. She said she would see us on Sunday when we got back. I just couldn't believe that she wouldn't be standing there in her kitchen as always with a big welcoming smile on her face when we walked in.

My chest felt like a ton of bricks was crushing it as we made our way into the house. Friends were milling around everywhere, and for the first time, I met Donna's ex, Sharon. Overcome with grief, she sat in the corner of the family room surrounded by the memories of their twenty-five years together.

Donna hadn't shown up for her golf game that morning. The one that I usually played with her when I wasn't working or Robin wasn't visiting. When she didn't show up for the game, her golfing buddies knew something had to be wrong; there was no way that Donna would miss her tee time. After trying several times to call her from a clubhouse phone, they drove to her house and found her on the kitchen floor. There was no doubt that she had died shortly after we left the previous Friday. They called the Sheriff and when no one knew what her intentions were, they called her ex. Apparently, Donna had not changed her will since she and Sharon had gone their separate ways, so it was left to Sharon to carry out Donna's last wishes.

Donna, knowing that she had cancer, told several of us that she wanted a simple funeral in the local Methodist church. She wanted Mahalia Jackson's old spiritual version of the song "A Rusty Old Halo" played, and she wanted some of her friends to sing "Amazing Grace." We used to tell her that none of us would be singing at her funeral and she could just get that out of her head. Of course, when we were all joking about it we never thought we would ever really have to make a decision like that.

Donna's group of close friends included a woman who could play almost anything by ear on the guitar. We didn't know if we could hold up to sing "Amazing Grace" without choking up, but three of us finally agreed that we owed it to our dear friend to try. Donna was probably smiling wherever she was, as we did our best to sing the song she had requested. The church was packed for her service, and then we drove behind the hearse one-hour-and-fifty-three minutes to Clovis, New Mexico where her parents were buried and where her plot was right next to their graves.

My semester was soon to be over, so Sharon, because she knew Donna would have wanted it, said that Patrick and I could stay at Donna's as long as we wanted. Donna had left everything to Sharon. Personally, I don't think it was an oversight on Donna's part that her will somehow never got changed. She had loved and lived with Sharon for twenty-five years, and I don't think she ever thought of loving anyone else.

Chapter 8

Robin's semester was about over, too, but now that she was about to get her master's she was going to stay on at the university coaching girls volleyball. She moved out of student housing and we got a small house together across the street from a huge park. There weren't many jobs in that little dusty New Mexico desert town, but I finally landed one at the local dollar store.

Did I love Robin? Yes. Did I love her with absolute abandon like I had loved Kathleen? No. I didn't think I would ever love anyone like that again. Was I jaded? Well no, not exactly, but from my devastating experience with Kathleen I had learned that literally anything could happen. Kathleen and I had planned to spend the rest of our lives together, but, instead, she had been forced to marry a man. A man I was positive she didn't love. I was running from the law. There was nothing about either one of our lives that even faintly resembled what we had planned for ourselves when we were so happy together.

But, to the extent I could allow myself to be happy, Patrick and I were happy living with Robin. Of course, there was the constant fear of Scott or the FBI finding us. That very real possibility never left our minds.

Both my Uncle Bob, the man who went crazy at his sister's funeral when her son admitted he was gay, and my paternal grandmother, who I loved with all my heart, died during the period we were on the run. I did not go back for either of their funerals for fear the authorities would be waiting for me. Midget told me later that the FBI had indeed been asking questions as to my whereabouts at my grandmother's funeral. Fortunately, none of the family except my mother and Midget knew where we were, and I was sure I could trust both of them not to reveal our location.

Fear of the unknown can make your life crazy. A feeling of dread hovered over me most of the time, and there were countless nights when I lay awake just waiting for the worst to happen. Whenever Robin and I went out to a restaurant, I would not be seated unless I could face the door. I literally could not stomach turning my back to the door for fear someone would walk up on me without my seeing him first.

Living with suspicion was a routine part of our daily lives. Robin and I both were constantly on the lookout for anything that was out of the ordinary in our neighborhood, at church, or at work. An unknown car parked across the street, or someone we didn't know talking to my manager at work made me so paranoid that I would be sick enough to have to go throw up.

I hoped against hope that the laws would change back again so that we could quit running. There was some talk in the Kentucky legislature about repealing the ruling that had made me a kidnapper in the eyes of the law. I prayed daily that the law would be repealed. While my type of kidnapping crime was low on the totem pole as far as the FBI was concerned, I knew Scott would be relentless in pushing the authorities to find us.

My mother kept up with the news in Paducah. According to her letters, Scott had done very well for himself since Patrick and I left. Our divorce had finally gone through in my absence, and Scott married a young waitress who he had been sleeping with who had worked for us in the second restaurant we'd opened there. He won a seat in the state legislature as the representative from McCracken County. Because I could find no attorney to represent me before I left, he had also taken literally all of our considerable assets and kept them for himself.

Chapter 9

In my mind, the only things I had really ever done were to be true to myself and try to raise and protect my son. Once I had discovered that I was a lesbian, I had to honor that recognition. For me, there had been no turning back, but Patrick and I both paid a very high price. We had been running for more than two years; I was tired of running and living life afraid of being discovered or turned in, but there was simply no choice.

We had been blessed to have caring, brave lesbians like Erin and Donna take us in, love us, and look out for us. The lesbians in the unofficial underground network who we met had kept us safe from Scott and the FBI. None of the lesbian mothers who had found safety and love in their care would ever forget their extreme courage and kindness.

They didn't have to do it, so what made them do it? The ones I knew had never had children, and yet they were devoted to a cause they saw as a gross injustice in our country. I never knew how these women communicated with each other to move the fugitives in their care from one safe house to the next. Erin told me once when I'd asked her to explain more about it that the less I knew, the better it would be for me.

Many lesbians I met during our years on the run had stuck with their husbands until their children were grown even though their relationships were a complete farce. Others, like me, had left their husbands and were running from place to place, never staying long enough to be traced. Still others were trying to fight for their children in court, which in the late sixties and early seventies was a total joke. Case after case was lost for no other reason than the mother was a lesbian.

But in spite of everything, Patrick and I had been very blessed. I am positive the lesbians who had sheltered and cared for us were the best humanity had to offer. And then there was Robin, who loved us both and was determined to make a life for us regardless of how dangerous it seemed to be at times.

Our life with Robin was stable and fun to the extent it could be under the circumstances. We rode horses almost every weekend. Some friends of ours from church had a small ranch outside of town where Robin taught Patrick and me how to ride. When Patrick was practicing his horsemanship, we rode in a freshly plowed field just in case he fell off. He did fall more than a couple of times, but Robin pitched him back in the saddle and soon he could hold his own with the rest of the kids.

One day while we were riding in the field, I challenged Robin to a horse race. I bet her a hamburger at a local fast food franchise that I could beat her in a race back to the barn. We lined our horses up on the edge of the field while Patrick served as our starter. He said, "Ready, set, go!" and off we went. We got off to a pretty fast start, but in the middle of the field, Robin's horse suddenly decided that he didn't like the whole idea of racing. The horse put on the brakes and pitched her over his head to soft dirt below.

As soon as I realized that I was racing all alone, I came back to help her, but to tell you the honest to God's truth, I couldn't keep myself from laughing. There was Robin, the consummate horsewoman, the one who had taught Patrick and me to ride, the one who was always so self-assured, and really the one who was always in control looking up at me completely covered in dirt.

There was so much dirt on her face that all I could see were the whites' of her eyes; she even had dirt in her teeth. She just could not have looked any funnier sprawled out like that, but I definitely should not have laughed. The devil must have made me do it. Though I must have apologized a hundred times or more, I don't think she ever forgave me for laughing like a wild hyena on dope.

Robin's neck and back were hurting and we were afraid to move her around too much. Patrick ran to the house and got our friends to come out and help us. We had to take her into town in the back of an old pickup truck over a washed-out gravel road. I had driven a stick shift before, but never anything like this one, so the ride over the old pot-holed road was a nightmare for Robin. The truck lurched and bucked all the way into town. If Robin hadn't already been banged up, she sure was after that ride.

Of course, it had to be a Sunday. The only medical help we could find was the local chiropractor who operated his practice out of his house. Fortunately, he was home and was able to tell us nothing was broken. He put everything back in place so we could get Robin home to some ice and a bed.

Robin considered Patrick her very own child, and she treated him that way. She felt a real responsibility for his upbringing; I could not have asked for a better partner to help raise my son. Robin kept him while I worked, and when she had classes to teach we scheduled it with my work so I could be home with Patrick.

I took some classes at the university and planned to continue my education at the next stop, which would be wherever Robin got a job teaching the next year. We had no idea where that would be, but we both thought that my getting an education had to be one of our most important priorities.

While we were waiting for a job opportunity for Robin, we both took Red Cross-sanctioned Lifeguard and Water Safety Instructor's classes at the university. The instructor had been a swimming coach for the U. S. Olympic team. He was a hard taskmaster. He taught both of the classes as if we were headed to the Summer Olympics in a couple of months. Honestly, he just about killed us both. Robin and I were just sure that he wanted to flunk the entire class.

One of the many requirements was that we had to swim a mile every night at the end of the class. One night I would be crying when I finished, and the next night Robin would be. Of course, after a few nights of what we thought was an unnecessarily grueling routine, we were in better shape and the required mile finally got to be a breeze.

As a final for the class, we had to rescue a thrashing drowning two-hundred-pound man. Can you imagine a one-hundred-and-ten-pound woman doing something like that? I can assure that it can be done, and all of my classmates yelled and clapped when I brought my simulated victim safely to the edge of the pool.

Chapter 10

A job for Robin opened up at the University of Montana. She would be coaching volleyball and teaching some PE classes and if we played our cards right, I could teach a lifeguard and Water Safety Instructor course or two. But most importantly, I could continue my education there at the university.

A feeling of impending doom had settled over us. By this time, we both knew that we desperately needed to move; I had become increasingly more afraid that we had stayed in this one place far too long. Although Robin's teaching job wouldn't start for three more months, we packed up and moved to Missoula early just to relieve some of our anxiety.

One of the other instructor's in Robin's department in Missoula had a small house to rent close to the university. Once we saw it, we fell in love with it. It literally had a white picket fence all the way around it and a big grassy yard for our son. We could actually have a puppy for Patrick, and we both felt we would be safe, at least for awhile.

As we settled in and began to establish a routine in our wonderful new home, some of the gut-wrenching anxiety over staying too long at the last stop began to slowly melt away. Of course, we could never totally relax, but our new place in Montana was about as close as I ever got to feeling at peace since the horrible nightmare had begun almost three years before.

All three of us loved Montana with its huge tall trees, big wide-open sky, and friendly down-to-earth people. As soon as we got there, we started exploring the area. We hiked the Big "M," visited city parks, and even took Patrick on a hike in the Rattlesnake National Recreation Area.

One of our brand new friends was a Biology professor at the university. She and the instructor we rented our house from were a lesbian couple, but, of course, they didn't introduce themselves that way. They were, instead, partners.

The professor volunteered every year to go out to the different wilderness area lakes to count the ducks and give the state wildlife department an idea of how many were nesting in that part of the state. Since we were new to the area, she thought it would be fun for all three of us, but especially for Patrick, to go with her on her annual volunteer job to assess the duck population. We were afraid we would be imposing, but she said no that, in fact, we could help carry the canoe where there wasn't enough water to float it.

It was a terrific excursion. Patrick practiced his numbers by counting the duck eggs when we found a nest unguarded by the mama duck. Lunch on those outings consisted of sandwiches, apples, and water. When it was time for lunch, we would pull the canoe up to one of the small islands in the middle of a lake. Then all of us would pile out, find a stump or a big old flat rock, and consume the vittles we brought. There is nothing quite like eating your food in Montana's great outdoors.

In the evenings, Robin and I played games with Patrick, let him draw or paint with his watercolors, or every now and then, we would all watch a cowboy show on TV. On most Sundays' Robin and Patrick read the funnies while I made pancakes. We found a kindergarten school for Patrick near the university where we would get him started when the semester began.

Robin was happy with the classes she had been assigned to teach, I would get to teach some classes, as well, and I would also be able to continue to work on getting my degree. It seemed like everything was clicking into place perfectly for us in Missoula.

Chapter 11

But in spite of all the good things we were being showered with, I started to begin to have an ominous sense that something terrible was about to happen. I just could not shake it even though, logically, there didn't seem to be a reason for the way I was feeling. At times, the dreadful feeling was almost suffocating. It got so bad that there were days when I begged Robin to pack us up so we could get away from there.

But when we sat down to calmly talk about what was going on with me, we both felt that maybe I'd been living under such a strain for so long that maybe I should seek counseling to help me get hold of my fear. Our talks made sense, and while they did ease my mind somewhat, my heart was still constantly waiting for the other shoe to drop.

To this day, I can still clearly recall as if it were yesterday every detail of what happened that Sunday morning. Patrick was five-and-a-half years old. It was 1970. Robin and Patrick were reading the funny papers in the front room on the new brown leather sofa we had purchased for our home. There was a knock at the front door. Robin and I froze; we never had company that early on Sunday morning. A neighbor might come to borrow a rake or something, but not that early. I hustled Patrick back to his bedroom and Robin went to answer the door.

At the door was a young black woman and two men dressed in suits. One of the men asked if Patrick and I lived there. Robin said, "Just a minute," and came to find me. Frightened almost witless, I went to the door. I immediately recognized Betty, the sitter who used to keep Patrick back when we lived with Scott in Paducah. The men were both FBI agents. As I looked past them to the dark gray sedan parked just beyond our white picket fence, I saw my ex-husband, Scott, sitting with a smug look on his face in the back seat of the FBI agents' car.

One of the agents told me that Scott was prepared to drop the kidnapping charge as long as I let him take Patrick back to Paducah. If I resisted, they would take Patrick anyway and arrest me for criminal parental kidnapping. There it was; it was all over as simple as that. My worst nightmare had finally come true on that beautiful Montana Sunday morning.

Betty came into the house. I knew that I had to do whatever I could to keep my composure; I simply could not break down in front of my son. He would be terrified, and we had to do everything we could to keep him as calm as possible. Robin and I talked to Patrick and told him that he was going on vacation with his dad and Betty. Robin packed a few of his things as the agents waited outside the front door.

Patrick didn't remember Scott or Betty. He said he didn't want to go and kept begging us not to make him go. He kept asking us, "Why can't I stay here with you and Robin, mommy?" He was sobbing uncontrollably as his little arms and legs were tightly wrapped around my legs. Finally, one of the agents came inside and literally pried him away from my legs. He put Patrick, kicking and screaming, under one arm and took him out to the waiting car. Betty left right behind them but stopped at the door, turned to me and said, "I'm sorry."

As the car pulled away from the curb, I could hear my little boy screaming over and over again. "Mommy, Mommy, Mommy!" His words ripped my heart right out of my chest. Robin grabbed me and led me to the sofa. I collapsed against her and began to wail for the loss of my little son. No amount of consoling helped. After what seemed like hours, thankfully and finally, numbness set in.

I could think of nothing except his precious little voice and his happy presence as I looked around the rooms. Patrick was what made our house a home. He made us a family. I simply didn't know if I could go on without him. Poor Robin's heart was breaking too, but she had to keep her wits about her in order to try and help me.

About 8:30 that same night, the phone rang. It was Betty; I could hear Patrick whimpering in the background. Betty told Robin that he had not stopped crying all day and the only way they could calm him down was to promise him that he could talk to me. I got to the phone in a flash and I can tell you for sure there has never been another sound sweeter than the voice of my small son.

As I was talking to my confused and terrified little boy, I began to discover my backbone again. It was what my Cherokee grandmother would have described as pure unadulterated gumption. I had made Patrick a promise that I would love him, care for him, and never leave him, and, by all that was in me, I was still going to find a way to keep my promise.

Scott might have the law on his side. For God sakes he even had the federal government doing his dirty work, but he did not have anything close to what I had. I had the inner conviction of absolutely knowing beyond a shadow of a doubt that what he had done from the first moment we had gotten Patrick up to and including what had happened that morning was, in truth, outrageously wrong.

I didn't care if every law and so-called Christian in the country was behind Scott. I had the sure knowledge that every thing that was really good and decent was behind me. Patrick deserved the best, and I knew in my heart that I was the best. I was his mother, and I was going to do whatever it took to right this situation. I had run all over the country trying to keep and protect Patrick, but now it was time for me to take a stand.

In the three years since Patrick and I had been gone from Paducah, Scott had somehow managed to become an elected public figure in the state of Kentucky. God only knows how he did it, but from my years living in that small town, I could make a darn good educated guess.

Scott did it the same way the rest of the crooked "good old boys" elected and maintained their local political offices in McCracken County. Even before I left Paducah, Scott was well entrenched with a powerful group of local politicians who held a virtual stranglehold on county politics. What you see in the movies about crooked small town politics is true. They scratched each other's backs and ran the county pretty much however they wanted. Through them, Scott was able to perpetrate a horrible injustice. The county Judge, his buddy, having only Scott's word that I was a lesbian, declared me an unfit mother and legally awarded temporary primary custody of Patrick to Scott, a man who didn't even want him.

Back then when men like the Mayor, the county Judge, and the Sheriff recommended someone for office, that candidate was almost a shoe-in to get elected. And the fact that Scott's dad was the minister of the largest Southern Baptist church in the county probably didn't hurt either. Yes, I'm sure that there had been rumors surrounding Scott's personal life, but nothing, of course, could be proven.

At election time, the rumors could even be attributed to lies broadcast by disgruntled opponents. He had remarried, and to all outward appearances just like the rest of the double-dealing local politicians, he had, on the surface, become a model citizen and a pillar of the community.

But I knew about some of the crooked things Scott had done to get where he was. I also knew that a politician's worst nightmare is to think that his dirty laundry might be exposed.

More than that, I had more grit than Scott ever thought about having. I would go back to Kentucky, but I wouldn't go as a beaten woman. I would go back to fight in court for my son.

Thank You!

If you have enjoyed this book, please tell your friends. If you have a chance, I would really appreciate an honest review.

Be sure to follow all the Mandy episodes and even get FREE Downloads and upcoming releases by visiting our website at http://thediscreetlesbian.com/.

All the best,
Mackenzie Stone

CPSIA information can be obtained at www.ICGtesting.com
Printed in the USA
LVOW08s0342030615

440870LV00029B/1276/P